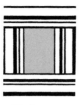

Privacy

PRIVACY

**Individual
Right v. Social
Needs**

Ted Gottfried

Issue and Debate
The Millbrook Press
Brookfield, Connecticut

Photos courtesy of Reuters/Bettmann: pp. 12, 18, 47, 57, 74;
Billy Rose Theatre Collection, New York Public Library: p. 21;
Wide World: pp. 25, 41; Ricky Flores/Impact Visuals: p. 31;
Bettmann: pp. 44, 54, 85; Photo Researchers: pp. 61 (© Joseph
Nettis), 90 (© Richard Hutchings); Rothco Cartoons: p. 71.

Library of Congress Cataloging-in-Publication Data
Gottfried, Ted.
Privacy : individual right v. social needs / by Ted Gottfried.
p.   cm.— (Issue and debate)
Includes bibliographical references and index.
Summary: Analyzes the controversial area of individual privacy
with a focus on such issues as the confidentiality of medical and
other personal information, the ethics of drug testing, the rights
of the news media to intrude into private lives, and the need to
balance law enforcement and privacy concerns.
ISBN 1-56294-403-7
1. Privacy, Right of—United States—Juvenile literature.
[1. Privacy, Right of.]   I. Title.   II. Series.
KF1262.Z9G68   1994   342.73'0858—dc20   [347.302858]
93-26791   CIP   AC

Published by The Millbrook Press
2 Old New Milford Road, Brookfield, Connecticut 06804

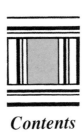

Contents

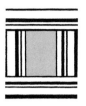

Privacy

The Right
Most Valued

The right to privacy was defined by U.S. Supreme Court Justice Louis Brandeis as "the right to be let alone . . . the right most valued by civilized men." [1] Much has changed since 1928, when those words were written. Progress and the pressures of the modern world have threatened individual privacy in ways Brandeis could not have imagined, and have forced us to re-examine this most valuable right from new perspectives. Privacy issues today are among the most fiercely contested of our time.

The right to privacy is difficult to define; legal scholars and others have long debated what it includes and even whether such a right exists. Unlike freedom of expression, which is protected by the First Amendment to the Constitution, privacy is not specifically safeguarded by the Bill of Rights or any other part of the Constitution. However, the Supreme Court and many legal scholars have found a basis for the right in various constitutional amendments.

The First Amendment, for example, protects freedom of association; courts have found that this implies the right to keep one's associations private. Also cited in support of the right to privacy are the Fifth Amendment, which prevents individuals from being forced to incriminate themselves; the Fourteenth Amendment, which guarantees "ordered liberty"; and the Ninth Amendment, which acknowledges that people have rights not specifically mentioned in the Constitution. But most often, a constitutional basis for the right to privacy is found in the Fourth Amendment, which protects people's homes and possessions from unreasonable searches and seizures.

These constitutional grounds for the right to privacy have been outlined in a range of court cases, creating what is called case law. In case law, court decisions (particularly decisions of the Supreme Court) become precedents; the principles that are outlined in them are followed in deciding subsequent cases. Case law evolves as precedents are re-examined and reinterpreted to fit new circumstances, and thus the law's view of privacy has changed over time and will likely continue to do so.

Some aspects of the right to privacy are also protected by written, or statute, laws. However, there is no broad U.S. statute that, like the non-binding Article Twelve of the Universal Declaration of Human Rights, states that "no one shall be subjected to arbitrary interference with his privacy, family, home, or correspondence." As we shall see in the following chapters, local and federal privacy laws are limited and address only a few of the many privacy issues that trouble people today.

Most of those issues touch on two broad questions. The first is the traditional one presented by Justice Brandeis: To what extent do individuals have a "right to be let alone"? The second is a newer question, made pressing by the computer age: To what extent can individuals control information about themselves once it has been released? In today's computer data banks, information that might once have been kept confidential is subject to retrieval, sharing, merging—and possible misuse.

While privacy issues crop up in many areas of life, this book will examine several areas of particular concern. One of these involves the news media. The media see an obligation to keep the public informed, and they often cite the free-press provision of the First Amendment as providing protection against interference in gathering news. But many people are disturbed by what they see as the intrusion by the media into the personal lives of people in the news—celebrities, politicians, people accused of crimes, and even victims of crime.

Law enforcement is a second area where privacy is an issue. Tools that police and other law enforcement agents use to catch criminals—wiretaps, hidden cameras, stop-and-frisk searches, examination of computer records, and the like—may invade the privacy of the innocent along with that of the guilty. How much privacy should the ordinary citizen have to give up to put the guilty behind bars? Many concerned with law enforcement and national security see dangers that justify stretching the boundaries of what is permitted. Others believe that pushing the limits of privacy is the greater danger.

Increasingly troubling are privacy issues involving matters such as contraception, abortion, and sexual preference. Does society have a right to interfere in the decisions people make in these most personal matters? Doctor-patient confidentiality and the confidentiality of health records are also being questioned. Should a pa-

Reporters crowd around film director Woody Allen during his 1993 child-custody dispute with actress Mia Farrow. The intense publicity surrounding the couple's breakup caused some people to question how far the media should intrude into celebrities' private lives.

tient's private records be fed into a database and shared for the public good? Should the records of children with AIDS be made available to school authorities?

Science is under pressure to help society solve its problems, and one of those problems is substance abuse. Testing for drugs and alcohol is becoming more and more common in government, transportation, and private industry. But the war against drugs has put privacy rights increasingly in the spotlight because such tests may infringe on the rights of employees. Advance notice of tests, selective and random testing, and observation of testing are some aspects of this issue.

An even more pressing concern may be the role of computers in eroding privacy. Once personal and financial records were kept in desks, file cabinets, and safes where they could be locked away. They were protected by laws covering searches and seizures. Today such records often become part of computer data banks that are accessible to the business community, credit agencies, political organizations, and government. The danger is pointed out by University of Illinois professor David F. Linowes: "With each new technological breakthrough, we become so carried away by the exciting new advances and expectations that we tend to ignore the sometimes harmful consequences that may ensue."[2]

Most of these issues affect young people as well as adults. For example, should schools be permitted to conduct random tests for drugs and alcohol? Who should have access to student records? May school officials search students or lockers without a warrant? Particularly in urban areas, the law today leans toward allowing such searches when a teacher or administrator has reason to suspect the presence of an illegal substance or a weapon.

In each of these areas, the right to privacy often comes in conflict with other rights and with the needs of society. Most people would agree that there are legitimate limits to privacy, but conflicts arise over what the limits are. The issues are not simply legal; they are matters of morals and ethics as well. They can be intense and emotional, and they can pit individuals against powerful social forces—the media, the government, employers, the banking and insurance industries, and, in the case of young people, parents and school authorities.

Finding a balance between competing rights and pressures is seldom easy, and few of us, teens or adults, are consistent in siding with one position. We tend to see our own privacy as inviolable and the next person's as subject to restrictions when it interferes with our own goals. The best we can do is strive for a fuller understanding of the issues, so that we can better weigh the conflicting needs of individuals and society in these cases. The following chapters may be of help in doing that.

Private
or Public:
Who Decides?

A free press is a highly valued American institution. Its ability to function without government interference is guaranteed by the First Amendment. Yet the rights of a free press and the privacy rights of individuals are frequently in conflict.

The people most often affected by this conflict fall into four groups. First are celebrities such as movie stars, sports personalities, and others whose profession involves attracting an audience. Second are national and community leaders—politicians, statesmen, business and labor leaders, military commanders—and those who are thrust into prominence by some outstanding deed or accomplishment. Third are people accused or convicted of crimes. Finally, there are crime victims—ordinary people on whom notoriety is imposed by circumstances.

Each of these categories presents different problems for the media with regard to questions of privacy. When it comes to celebrities, journalists often claim the widest leeway. They point out that entertainment and sports figures use the press more than they are exploited by it. Personally and through press agents, celebrities release stories that flatter them. The media accommodate them by running such stories. Much time on television and space in newspapers and magazines is devoted to these self-serving handouts.

This is as true today as it was thirty-odd years ago when Howard Rushmore, editor of the era's top-selling exposé magazine, *Confidential,* pointed out that "if we build them up, then we have an obligation to knock them down when they violate the image we have helped them create."[1] Rushmore was particularly concerned with revealing immoral actions that contradicted the wholesome images celebrities cultivated.

Most public personalities, however, feel that the fact that their talents or abilities draw public attention does not entitle the public to know all the details of their private lives. Before his recent death, world-famous ballet dancer Rudolf Nureyev expressed it this way: "There are certain signs every family, every person, is allowed to put outside his doorstep. *No trespassing.*"[2]

But the *Confidential* viewpoint has prevailed with such sensational media of today as the tabloid weekly *National Enquirer* and TV's *Inside Edition.* Attracting large audiences and thriving on scandal, they resolutely target big names like Woody Allen, Mia Farrow, Madonna, Sean Penn, Elizabeth Taylor, Warren Beatty, and many others. NBC commentator Maria Shriver has pointed out that "much of the mainstream press now feels the heat to follow in the tabloids' footsteps."[3]

The Character Issue. Nowhere is this more true than in politics, where the media invade privacy at the highest levels of government, including the White House itself. During the 1992 election campaign, both President

George Bush and Democratic candidate Bill Clinton were interrogated about extramarital affairs by reporters on camera. Both were outraged. Four years earlier, leading presidential candidate Senator Gary Hart had been driven from the race after photographers and reporters staked out the apartment of a woman with whom he was alleged to be having an adulterous relationship.

Do voters need to know this information? "If a man will cheat on his wife, he'll cheat on the country," proclaimed a Philadelphia woman interviewed during the 1992 presidential campaign.[4] But morality is not the only problem. If a leader lies or is evasive or less than truthful about personal matters, can he or she be trusted to level with the American people on crucial national issues? Fidelity aside, is not truthfulness a standard to which our leaders should be held?

In earlier times the media operated according to a so-called "gentleman's agreement" by which such transgressions as excessive drinking, gambling, and infidelity by public figures were not revealed. News stories of scandals involving presidents Warren Harding, Franklin Roosevelt, Dwight Eisenhower, John Kennedy, and Lyndon Johnson were suppressed. Only after these leaders' deaths were their frailities made public.

Today, however, the so-called character issue is widely seen as a public concern. Journalists insist that the people have a right to know the truth about their leaders and that they have a duty to provide it. If that means secretly following a presidential candidate to an extramarital rendezvous, then so be it.

But what about the leader's family? Are their private lives also legitimate subjects for scrutiny? And does this apply to the families of those at all levels of government and even to the families of those who are not in government but play a role in public affairs?

*The "character issue": At a 1992 press
conference, Gennifer Flowers reveals what
she said was a twelve-year-long affair with
Bill Clinton, then a candidate for president.*

Phyllis Schlafly does not think so. Schlafly is a prominent conservative Republican who played a key role in drawing up the Republican platform for the 1992 presidential election and in retaining its anti-abortion language. She is both a spokeswoman for and a symbol of the "family values" proclaimed at the 1992 Republican national convention.

Shortly after the convention, in September 1992, with the election less than two months off, Ms. Schlafly's forty-one-year-old son John revealed his homosexuality to the *San Francisco Examiner*. He had previously been "outed" (identified as a homosexual) by gay journalists eager to point up the inconsistency between his lifestyle and his mother's "family values." Ms. Schlafly saw the revelation as "a political hit on me . . . because of my success in the Republican platform."[5]

Undoubtedly, she was right. At the same time, it was not her privacy which had been breached, but her son's. Not a public figure himself, was John Schlafly fair game for the press?

Legally, he probably was. Courts distinguish between libel, in which damaging falsehoods have been published about someone, and invasion of privacy, in which the truth may have been revealed against a person's will. The legal guidelines for invasion of privacy cases are weighted in favor of the press; courts still rely mostly on *Time, Inc.* v. *Hill* (1967).

News or Entertainment? The case involved a family, the Hills, held hostage by three escaped convicts for nineteen hours in 1952. Subsequently a novel, *The Desperate Hours*, fictionalized the incident. Two years after the book was published, it was adapted as a Broadway play. When *Life* magazine reviewed the play, it described the incidents in it as true and linked them with the Hill family by name. The Hills had long since moved from the home where their ordeal had taken place, but *Life* nevertheless photographed the play's performers in that setting. They were posed to show some of the more violent incidents in the play, admitted exaggerations of what had actually occurred.

The Hill family sued under a New York State right-of-privacy statute permitting newsworthy persons to recover damages upon proving that an account was fictionalized. They won the case, and a state appeals court affirmed the verdict. But the United States Supreme Court, in a 6–3 decision, reversed it.[6]

Writing for the majority, Justice William J. Brennan, Jr., pointed out that the topic of the *Life* piece was "a matter of public interest." He added that it would be a "grave risk" to media freedom "if we saddle the press with the impossible burden of verifying to a certainty the facts associated in news articles with a person's name, picture or portrait . . ."[7] In effect, this decision granted the media the widest latitude in interpreting the facts of any case once those facts had become public. Critics of the decision feel that it opened the door to "docudramas" and "faction"—the blurring of actual events and fiction, as in the television dramatizations of the 1993 Waco siege and other news events.

Such dramatizations are of course several steps removed from the initial media coverage of the case. Most crime reporters are professionals who take very seriously their responsibilities to the public, to law enforcement, and to the legal system. On many occasions they cooperate with police by holding back on stories, even foregoing "scoops," while an investigation is in progress.

A scene from the Broadway play The Desperate Hours. *A review of the play, blending fact and fiction, gave rise to an important right-to-privacy lawsuit.*

Nevertheless, it is a fact of their calling that stories about crimes of passion, violence, and murder sell newspapers and increase TV ratings. They must often decide between conscience and an ongoing pressure to sensationalize. Frequently crime coverage blurs the line between news and entertainment.

Suspects in lurid crimes come under intense scrutiny from the media. Family members, neighbors, co-workers, and friends are interviewed, and their statements appear in the newspapers and on TV. School records are examined, job attendance is checked, former spouses and lovers are tracked down. All this and more is reported to the public.

By penetrating the privacy of the accused, the media flesh out an image. That image becomes identified with the crime itself, especially when the crime is violent. The accused and the crime are merged in the public mind. Many defense attorneys fear that the result is prejudice against defendants, who should be presumed innocent until proven guilty in a court of law.

Also, the media may reveal things unrelated to the crime that the suspect might rather not have made public. A youthful offense, a painful divorce, an illness, a flare-up of temper, unsatisfactory job performance, treatment for depression—everybody has something they would rather others didn't know about.

Media Guidelines. Weighing whether or not to disclose such information can be one of the most difficult decisions for a reporter. Many media organizations have guidebooks for personnel, but they tend to focus on guarding against legal action rather than on the issues of ethics that may be involved. The Associated Press, for example, advises that "when a person becomes involved in a news event, voluntarily or involuntarily, he forfeits the right to privacy. Similarly, a person some-how involved in a matter of legitimate public interest . . . normally can be written about with safety.'' In fairness, the AP does warn against ''a story or picture that dredges up the sordid details of a person's past and has no current newsworthiness.''[8]

But what if the details are not sordid, but neverthe-less reveal facts someone may not want revealed, things that will affect the person's life? This was what hap-pened in 1965 when *New York Times* reporter McCan-dlish Phillips was assigned to investigate the back-ground of the anti-Semitic head of the New York State Ku Klux Klan, Daniel Burros. Phillips learned that Bur-ros had been born into a Russian-Jewish immigrant fam-ily and had been bar mitzvahed as a Jew.

When Phillips confronted Burros with these facts, the KKK leader threatened to shoot the reporter and to blow up the *New York Times* building if the paper ran the story. Implying suicide, he said, ''I'm going to go out in a blaze of glory.'' Phillips took these threats very seriously and tried to reason with Burros, telling him that he had ''to break the grip fascism has on you.''[9]

Burros was unmoved. Despite his concern, Phillips wrote the story and the *Times* printed it. After it ap-peared, Burros killed himself with a bullet to the heart followed by a second shot to the head.

Subsequently, the *Times* received letters condemn-ing the newspaper for invading the privacy of the Klan leader. Even some journalists felt that Burros had obvi-ously been mentally unstable and that the paper should not have run a story that might push him into suicide. Phillips himself felt very bad about what had happened, but was sure that both his own handling of the story and the publication of it had been the right thing to do.

It was a matter of the public's right to know. But

just how far does this right extend? Are there cases where privacy should take precedence?

For instance, in rape cases where stigma may attach to the victim, should identity be kept confidential? And if the victim's private life is exposed in court, should the press refrain from making it public knowledge?

In the case of William Kennedy Smith, *The New York Times* and NBC News did not refrain. Smith, a nephew of Senator Edward Kennedy, was accused of the late-night rape of a woman at his family's Palm Beach estate. Both the *Times* and NBC revealed the name of the woman. They subsequently divulged many details of her private life, including some related to her children, her parents, and her relationships with men.

Previously it had been common practice not to name rape victims. Michael G. Gartner, the president of NBC News, explained why his organization broke with that custom in the Palm Beach case. "It was not an easy decision," he said. "We had named the accused without any of that debate at all, just automatically named him. It's really a question of fairness and balance." [10]

When Smith was found innocent, Gartner's point seemed validated to many in the media. However, NBC also named the victim in the rape trial of former heavyweight champion boxer Mike Tyson, who was found guilty. Gartner's view remained that "you have to look at this on a case-by-case basis. It really comes down to one issue. What is the fair thing to do?" [11]

Keith Ensey believes naming the accuser is fair. On May 9, 1991, the University of Rhode Island student was accused by a young woman he knew of kidnapping her at gunpoint and raping her. However, Keith was a thousand miles away in Chicago when the alleged crime

After William Kennedy Smith was acquitted of rape charges in 1991, many people questioned the intense publicity that surrounded the case.

took place and could prove it. His accuser subsequently admitted that she had made up the story.

By then the media had run Keith's picture, related details of the alleged crime, and gone into his background and personality. "Everyone will always think of me as either the kid who raped that girl, or the kid who was accused of rape," Keith said after his innocence had been established. "The media did that." He added, "If they're going to put out the name of the accused, they have to put out the victim's name. It's only fair."[12]

Those concerned about crimes against women strongly disagree. They say that many rape victims decline to prosecute because of their fear of publicity. They contend that when the press reveals a victim's identity, many other victims are influenced not to bring charges and perpetrators go free.

The situation is even more complicated when the victim is a minor. When a family-owned Washington State newspaper, the weekly *Shelton Mason County Journal,* named a ten-year-old sexual assault victim and gave details of the crime, local residents were outraged. Demonstrations against the paper led State Senator Tim Sheldon to push a bill through the legislature prohibiting the press from naming minors in sex assault cases. The constitutionality of the law, however, is questionable. In *Cox Broadcasting Corporation* v. *Cohn* (1975), the United States Supreme Court struck down a Georgia law forbidding the media to name rape victims. Whether the Court might rule differently in a case where the victim is a minor remains to be seen.

In the Washington case, the ten-year-old victim had been teased and ostracized by classmates after her identity was made known. However, Charles Gay, managing editor of the offending newspaper, opposed the legislation. "We are better off in finding out what happened in our community in the case of this crime," he maintained. "You don't reinforce society's stigma by leaving names out and failing to cover trials." Gay insisted that "the principle involved of fair coverage is the same whether the person is twenty-five, or ten." [13]

Despite this view of "fair coverage" and the precedent of the *Cox* v. *Cohn* case which supports it, newspapers may find their coverage of such cases restricted in future on other grounds. In *Wolston* v. *Reader's Digest Association, Inc.* (1979), the Supreme Court narrowed the definition of just who is a "public figure" and therefore fair game for the press. Writing for the majority, Justice William H. Rehnquist (later Chief Justice) pointed out that a "private individual is not automatically transformed into a public figure just by becoming involved in or associated with a matter that attracts public attention." [14] As a rule it is up to the lower courts to decide who falls into the category of "public figure" in each case.

The questions we have considered in this chapter are not easy ones. A free press may infringe on privacy. An absolute right to privacy may undermine the freedom of the press. The downside to every right is that it may interfere with another right.

Prosecution or Persecution?

Violent crime is a major concern of the American people. They want organized crime bosses and drug kingpins prosecuted, convicted, and jailed. They want police to take back neighborhoods from crack dealers, muggers, and hoodlums. They want the war on crime to be finally won. This puts pressure on those who fight the war and pushes them to stretch the limits of their authority. Sometimes they are accused of trampling on citizens' rights—including the right to privacy.

Privacy would seem to be protected from police intrusion by the Fourth Amendment to the Constitution, which prohibits "unreasonable searches and seizures" and insists on "probable cause" for the issuing of a warrant "describing the place to be searched, and the persons or things to be seized." When it was written, the amendment was intended to protect people from the type of house-to-house searches British soldiers had conducted during colonial times. In a series of court cases, however, Fourth Amendment protection was applied first to property outside the home and then to persons—their thoughts, beliefs, and communications—as well as to property.

"The Knock on the Door." In 1914, in the case of *Weeks* v. *United States,* the Supreme Court ruled that evidence seized without a warrant could not be used in court. Over the next fifty years this prohibition was confirmed and came to be known as the exclusionary rule. This was in keeping with the view expressed by Supreme Court Justice Felix Frankfurter in *Wolf* v. *Colorado* (1949), that "the security of one's privacy against arbitrary intrusion by the police is basic to a free society." Frankfurter added, "The knock on the door, whether by day or night, as a prelude to a search, without authority of law but solely on the authority of the police [is] . . . inconsistent with the conception of human rights."[1]

Beginning in the 1970s, however, a series of Supreme Court decisions weakened the privacy safeguards of the exclusionary rule. Among the issues raised was that of "stop and frisk" searches, in which police stop and search individuals for "probable cause" without getting a warrant. The Court held that in certain circumstances "stop and frisk" principles may also apply to vehicles, business premises, and even homes. Stanley N. Katz, a professor at Princeton University, wrote that these extensions of "stop and frisk" were "ominous hints that the Court may do away with the Fourth Amendment exclusionary rule."[2]

Some law enforcement officials would like to see that happen. While civil liberties advocates have been concerned that the Court "has limited the kinds of judicial proceedings in which the exclusionary rule can be applied,"[3] tough-minded law-and-order champions have worried that the exclusionary rule has tied the hands of police and have applauded decisions restricting it.

Today accusations of police intrusions into privacy often come from members of ethnic and racial minorities, who charge that biased attitudes lead to routine violations of privacy. One publicized case involved 125 African-American students at the State University of New York (SUNY) at Oneonta. In September 1992, a seventy-seven-year-old Oneonta woman was stabbed during a burglary attempt. She identified her assailant as a young black man and said he had cut his hand while attacking her, but she could provide no further identification. The police contacted the vice president of the SUNY campus, who gave them the names and addresses of 125 male African-American students. Police officers then tracked the students down and questioned them; as one student described it, "They came to my dorm, asked me where I was the night before, and demanded to see my hands."[4]

The students protested that their privacy was invaded in two ways: The university had no right to share their names and addresses with the police, and the police had no right to breach the privacy of their homes and persons (by demanding to examine their hands) without warrants and with no more probable cause than skin color. SUNY/Oneonta president Alan B. Donovan agreed, deploring the "violation of the privacy of our students."[5] However, there are people who are deeply concerned about increases in violent crime and believe the police must violate privacy to some extent to bring lawbreakers to justice. In their view, the purpose of the Oneonta investigation—to remove a knife-wielding criminal from society—would justify the invasion of privacy.

Police patrol a neighborhood in New York City. Minority groups have charged that prejudice is behind many police intrusions of privacy.

Wiretapping and Surveillance. Much of the debate over privacy and law enforcement has focused on surveillance techniques, especially wiretapping. In 1967, the Supreme Court ruled that warrantless wiretapping violates the Fourth Amendment. This case, *Katz* v. *United States*, tried to set a standard that could be used in similar cases, calling on law enforcement agencies and courts to weigh the benefits of surveillance against an individual's "reasonable expectation of privacy."[6] But the standard proved difficult to apply, partly because it is hard to determine what constitutes a "reasonable expectation."

Laws regulating wiretapping have tried to be more specific. For example, in the 1968 Crime Control and Safe Streets Act, Congress authorized the use of wiretaps and other electronic eavesdropping devices by federal agents. The law required agents to secure a warrant and limit the electronic surveillance to the areas and goals covered by the warrant. Those concerned about privacy rights believe that any information obtained otherwise should be inadmissible as evidence. The courts, however, have been lenient in interpreting the law. They have taken the position that just because evidence of a crime obtained by wiretapping, electronic "bugging," hidden cameras, or other devices was stumbled upon accidentally in the course of an investigation with different goals, that is no reason to exclude it. In case after case, federal judges have ruled that justice would not be served by so rigid an interpretation.[7]

Electronic surveillance was an issue in the 1992 trial of John Gotti in New York. Gotti, long alleged by the media to be a major figure in organized crime, was tried under a racketeering conspiracy law that enabled thirteen charges to be grouped together in one indictment. Among the counts of which he was convicted were murder, conspiracy to commit murder, extortion, illegal gambling, obstruction of justice, and tax fraud. Much of the evidence presented against him in court had been obtained by hidden surveillance devices, which were used to keep both Gotti and many of his confederates under constant scrutiny. Their phones were tapped; listening devices were placed in their homes, offices, and in places where they socialized; and hidden cameras tracked their movements. Their associates were investigated, and sometimes they too were placed under surveillance. Throughout the trial the defense raised repeated objections that the investigation had gone far beyond the scope of what various warrants authorized, but efforts to have the evidence disallowed were for the most part unsuccessful.

One of the places where government agents had hidden listening devices was De Robertis Pasticceria, a popular dessert cafe in New York's East Village. Many of Gotti's associates were regulars there, stopping by two or three times a week for coffee and pastry or lemon ices. The bugs were hidden in the old-fashioned booths lining the rear of the establishment.

Innocent customers were also recorded. Was their privacy violated? Suppose evidence had been uncovered of a completely unrelated crime, committed by one of those inadvertently bugged. Should that evidence be admissible in court? Should it be allowed in a civil suit? What if it were leaked to the press, or to a member of the taped person's family? What if it is never used at all? Has the right to privacy of the person taped been any the less violated? The courts have not been consistent in dealing with these questions.

Some people hold that if breaches of privacy by law enforcement agencies can be excused by the need to fight organized crime, then surely they must be justifiable when it comes to national security. In the early 1970s, federal agents put many antiwar protesters under surveillance on the grounds that their activities hindered the conduct of the undeclared war we were waging in Vietnam. Their mail was scrutinized, their telephone calls were monitored, their activities were photographed, and sometimes even their conversations were recorded. Later, when this surveillance was revealed, some activists obtained their records under the federal Freedom of Information Act and sued the government on the grounds that their privacy had been invaded. Many won their suits.

Not everybody agrees that they should have won. Some still view the Vietnam era's antiwar protesters as having engaged in activity counter to the best interests of their country. They think federal agents were completely justified in keeping them under the strictest surveillance. The right to privacy, they believe, must take a backseat in wartime. National security must come first.

Whether the goal is fighting crime or preserving national security, a rapidly expanding technology makes it easier for law enforcement authorities to penetrate privacy. There have even been attempts to shape technology toward that end. One such effort focuses on the switchover by telephone companies from standard analog transmission to digital communications and fiber-optic cables. Conventional wiretapping can pick up voices on the analog lines, but the Federal Bureau of Investigation says it would record only a hiss on a digital line and only silence on a fiber-optic line.[8]

In April 1992 the FBI proposed legislation requiring telephone equipment to be standardized for wiretapping. Extensive modifications of the equipment would be necessary, and the cost would be passed on to customers. One advantage of the changes would be that law enforcement agents could monitor calls from remote sites, instead of splicing into lines leading directly to the phone being tapped. The FBI had hoped to find a congressional sponsor for the bill by spring of 1993, but that didn't happen.

One reason was a 1993 study by the federal government's General Services Administration, which concluded that "equipment already exists that can be used to wiretap the digital communications lines." The report sharply criticized the FBI and warned that the proposal would "make it easier" for criminals and spies and terrorists "to electronically penetrate the phone network."[9]

Meanwhile, other high-tech gadgets are already being used by many local, state, and federal law enforcement agencies. Computer-sorted phone taps can pick out one voice from all those using a phone company system and record its conversations. Satellites developed by the Defense Department can track stolen cars electronically. Parolees subject to curfew are receiving phone calls from computers that recognize their voices and confirm their identity. Tiny video cameras can be installed in telephone mouthpieces and use existing phone wires to transmit an image to law enforcement screens.[10]

Not all police officials approve of the gadgetry. Police Chief Joseph McNamara of San Jose, California, believes that "the potential for abuse of these types of devices is so great that they must be controlled. He adds that "the stuff can be anathema to privacy rights."[11]

One gadget that may pose a particular threat to privacy has already started to be used. It is the Unmanned Aerial Vehicle (UAV) and is about the size of a Frisbee. These miniature pilotless aircraft will fly high above the ground and will contain high-resolution cameras, infrared detectors, and sensors capable of detecting illegal narcotics. The U.S. Border Patrol has already used them to zero in on illegal aliens and drug-smuggling operations.

One UAV model, the Pointer, can be launched by one person and will stay in the air for an hour. During that time it can monitor activity over an entire neighborhood. It is cheaper than a police helicopter, doesn't put a pilot's life at risk, and isn't easy to detect from the ground.

The problem, according to civil libertarians, is that UAVs would bring the ordinary citizen under surveillance along with the perpetrators of crimes. Janlori Goldman, director of the American Civil Liberties Union Privacy Project, points out that such surveillance would be performed without a warrant, which would make it "an infringement on privacy rights."[12]

Less flashy than the UAVs, but equally controversial, is electronic fingerprinting. This transforms a thumbprint, for instance, into a series of electronic impulses that can be read by scanners. The print might be embedded in a credit card that can be read by scanners feeding into a computer for an instant check. Eventually, however, embedding the print may not be necessary. If the thumb has held the card, that may be enough for high-sensitivity scanners.

In California, welfare applicants' fingerprints were checked this way to prevent them from collecting duplicate benefits. The program virtually put an end to such "double-dipping." It saved the state $7.8 million over sixteen months, and 314 violators were caught. Nevertheless, critics believe that forcing people to be fingerprinted in order to collect benefits violates their privacy rights and may put them in the position of incriminating themselves. They successfully lobbied the New York

State legislature to pass a law forbidding the sharing of welfare records with the criminal justice system.

But when it comes to police use of new surveillance technology, many states neither prohibit nor regulate breaches of privacy. Evidence obtained by the most far-reaching surveillance methods is admitted in their courts. And in states that require a court order for electronic surveillance, or forbid wiretapping altogether, police officers and private investigators routinely circumvent the law and use such methods anyway. Usually the state courts have allowed the results to be admitted as evidence. The Supreme Court has so far refused to reverse state convictions based on electronic data admitted in state trials.

The Victim's Privacy. Many prosecutors favor easing rules of evidence, but sometimes this can affect the victim as well as the perpetrator.

This happened during a 1992–1993 trial in New Jersey. The defendants were four Glen Ridge high school football players charged with sexually assaulting a retarded seventeen-year-old woman. State Judge Burrell Ives Humphreys, in a series of pre-trial rulings, decided that defense attorneys were entitled to have access to the woman's medical records, including information having to do with her previous sexual activity, and to introduce some of it into evidence.

Previously, under New Jersey law, such information was considered confidential, and trial juries were not allowed to hear it. But Judge Humphreys decreed that "confidentiality and privilege must give way when they conflict with rights to a fair trial. All privileges are barriers to the truth." [13]

Attorney Vincent Kramer, representing the victim

and her parents, said this was the first time a New Jersey judge had overturned patient-doctor confidentiality in a case involving sexual assault. "The records are confidential and no one on this earth is entitled to see them," he declared.[14]

But just what is private in terms of defendants' need to exonerate themselves? Many feel with attorney Kramer that the courts go too far in allowing the victim's privacy to be violated. They point to the 1988 murder trial of Robert Chambers, in which the private diary of his victim, nineteen-year-old Jennifer Levin, was admitted into evidence. The details, widely covered by the media, caused great pain to the bereaved Levin family. (Chambers pleaded guilty to first-degree manslaughter.)

What are the limits? Should privacy take a backseat to courtroom justice? To fighting crime? To national security? Or should it be granted the status accorded it in the Universal Declaration of Human Rights affirming that "no one shall be subjected to arbitrary interference with his privacy"?[15]

Intimacy and Intrusion

The privacy questions concerning many Americans today have to do with being free from intrusion by government and others in the most personal matters. These include marital and extramarital behavior, birth control practices, sexual orientation, and the reading and viewing of pornographic materials. At the head of the list is the debate over abortion, between pro-choice and pro-life advocates. Pro-choice insists that a woman's right to privacy includes her right to choose to have an abortion without interference. Pro-life says that society's obligation to preserve the fetus (which they consider an unborn child) takes precedence over privacy.

For more than twenty years, the Supreme Court decision that has dominated the controversy has been *Roe v. Wade* (1973). To understand the privacy issues involved we must first look at that decision and at what it does and does not say. It refused, for instance, to "resolve the difficult question of when life begins." On the other hand, it noted that "person" as used in the Constitution and the Fourteenth Amendment "does not include the unborn," which meant that the rights these documents guaranteed did not apply to fetuses. In the broadest sense, this wording is understood to mean that a woman's right to the privacy of her body takes precedence over the right to life of the unborn infant.

Justice Harry A. Blackmun, writing the majority opinion, pointed out that "the Constitution does not explicitly mention any right of privacy." However, he added that in *Roe* v. *Wade* "the Court has recognized that a right of personal privacy . . . does exist under the Constitution" and that it "is broad enough to encompass a woman's decision whether or not to terminate her pregnancy." That seemed pretty clear, but the decision went on to deliberately leave a loophole by acknowledging that "some State regulation in areas protected by the right is appropriate. . . . The privacy right involved, therefore, cannot be said to be absolute." [1]

Questions About Roe. Obviously the wording of *Roe* v. *Wade* left many questions unanswered, questions that are still being fought over today. If the "right of privacy" is not "absolute," then it is open to interpretation by both sides in the abortion controversy. The issues this raises are personal and painful, and frequently much more complex than the arguments of either side acknowledge. For instance:

Should a woman have to get the father's consent to have an abortion, or is she entitled to make the decision alone?

"Only one of the two marriage partners can prevail," was the Supreme Court's decision in 1976. "Since it is the woman who physically bears the child . . . the balance weighs in her favor." [2] Not so, protest the right-to-lifers. The unborn child, they say, is the re-

Anti-abortion protesters are arrested after trying to block access to a clinic. The debate over abortion has sparked strong feelings on both sides.

sult of an act of love involving two people. Each should have equal input into the decision.

Shall parents of pregnant minors have veto power over the inherently private decision not to have the baby?

In 1976 the Supreme Court said no.[3] The pro-choice position was expressed by the Court in that decision, which said that "any independent interest the parent may have in the termination of the minor daughter's pregnancy is no more weighty than the right of privacy of the competent minor mature enough to have become pregnant."[4] The other side responded that the pregnancy is proof not of maturity, but of immaturity, proving the need for parental guidance and intervention.

In 1981 the Court ruled that state law might require a doctor to inform a teenaged woman's parents before performing an abortion if the adolescent was still living at home and dependent on them.[5] In 1992 the Court said a pregnant teenager could be compelled to notify one parent—but not necessarily both—as long as there was a provision allowing her to obtain permission for an abortion from a judge instead.[6]

Must an adult who has decided on an abortion go through a waiting period and receive pro-life counseling before being allowed to proceed, or does this requirement infringe on her privacy?

In 1983, and again in 1986, the Court said no.[7] In the first case, the Court said she did not have to wait twenty-four hours after being told that "the unborn child is a human life from the moment of conception" before having the operation.[8] In the second, they struck down a requirement that she be given "informed consent" information phrased to discourage abortions.[9]

Pro-life supporters argue that "informed consent" means simply bringing the woman face-to-face with the life-and-death nature of her decision and that a waiting period simply provides time to consider it fully. Opponents stick to the argument that it is a *private* decision and should not be subject to unwanted and state-enforced pressure to change it. In 1992 the Court upheld a Pennsylvania law requiring twenty-four-hour waiting periods.

Privacy and Morality. Questions of morality abound in the abortion debate. But such questions were raised long before *Roe* v. *Wade*. From the beginning, the states of the United States passed laws that regulated the most private behavior. Such laws have banned extramarital sex, dictated what activities were allowable between husband and wife, forbade gay and lesbian relationships, and spelled out what could be read or viewed in the privacy of one's home or discussed in a doctor's office.

Many—but not all—of these laws could no longer be enforced following the Supreme Court's decision in the 1965 case of *Griswold* v. *Connecticut*.[10] The two laws at issue in the case have been described by Professor Paul Bender of the University of Pennsylvania Law School as "an old and little-used statute that prohibited the use of contraceptives, and another statute that made the aiding or abetting of such an offense a crime."[11] When Planned Parenthood tried to open a birth control clinic in New Haven, Connecticut, its personnel were convicted of "aiding and abetting married persons in using contraceptives."[12]

Setting aside the conviction, the Supreme Court said that "marriage is . . . intimate to the degree of being sacred."[13] Writing the majority opinion, Justice William O. Douglas asked, "Would we allow the police to search the sacred precincts of marital bedrooms for

An early activist in the fight for birth control, Kitty Marion, sells pamphlets in this 1915 photo.

telltale signs of the use of contraceptives? The very idea is repulsive to the notions of privacy surrounding the marriage relationship.''[14]

But this raises a question that has never been resolved by the courts and probably never will be: If an immoral act is performed privately, does that make it any the less immoral?

Many sincere people of different religions believe that the use of contraception is a sin. Some advocate bringing back laws making distribution of contraceptive devices and information illegal. When they are met with the argument that this is a private matter and that today, in the age of AIDS, perhaps it is a matter of public health as well, they answer in terms of their deeply held moral convictions. Abstinence, they say, is the only ethical means of birth control.

They are not alone in challenging privacy on the basis of morality. Such challenges come from many different—and sometimes unexpected—directions. ''Privacy is an unpopular right among some feminists,'' according to Wendy Kaminer, author of *Fearful Freedom: Women's Flight from Equality*. She goes on to explain that this is because claims of privacy have frequently been used to hide crimes of wife battering and child abuse.[15] ''Secrecy contributes to child abuse'' was the *Los Angeles Times* summation of the expert testimony at an April 1992 hearing of the U.S. Advisory Board on Child Abuse and Neglect.[16] However, agreeing with the eighteenth-century common-law principle that ''a man's house is his castle,'' the police have often backed off from interfering in domestic disputes. Kaminer sees this as one reason ''why so much feminist energy has gone into making the private public, the personal political.''[17]

In one example of this, anti-pornography activists have called privacy rights into question in their crusade.

They say there is a direct connection between pornography and violent sex crimes against women. They want such material banned and make no exceptions for the private reading or viewing of pornography in one's own home. These arguments helped win passage of strict anti-pornography laws in both Minneapolis and Indianapolis. The Supreme Court subsequently found both laws to be unconstitutional.

The Court has seesawed over privacy and pornography, granting different weights to Fourth Amendment implications of privacy. In *Stanley* v. *Georgia* (1969), it confirmed citizens' right to read obscene books or watch X-rated motion pictures in the privacy of their homes.[18] But in *Osborne* v. *Ohio* (1990), the Court said that right did not apply to child pornography.[19]

Privacy advocates say anyone should be able to look at anything in the seclusion of their own home no matter how loathsome or pornographic it may be. Their opponents say that because such material creates attitudes that result in violent acts against women it should be forbidden. Here morality is backed up by a claim of danger. But civil libertarians see the real threat being to privacy. This view is behind such federal laws as the 1984 Cable Communications Policy Act and the 1988 Video Privacy Protection Act, which set tight restrictions on the release of records of cable television subscriptions and videocassette rentals.

Another source of danger to privacy are certain gay and lesbian groups that, frustrated by society's prejudice against homosexuality, have resorted to ''outing'' (exposing prominent gays and lesbians who have kept their sexual preference private). The theory is that if top athletes, actors and actresses, and other celebrities admired by the public are shown to be gay or bisexual, then society will more quickly move to accept lesbians and gays who are less well known.

Gay veterans march in front of the White House in 1993, during the debate over the ban on homosexuals in the military.

In 1993 gays and lesbians were confronted by right-to-privacy arguments in the furor over doing away with the regulation banning their service in the military. General Colin L. Powell, then chairman of the Joint Chiefs of Staff, said that lifting the ban "would be detrimental to good order and discipline for a variety of reasons, principally relating around the issue of privacy."[20] Navy leaders expressed concern about sailors at sea, who live in such close quarters that those who are openly gay may, by their presence alone, interfere with the privacy of heterosexuals. Commander Craig Quigley, speaking for the Navy, worried that heterosexual men showering with men they knew to be gay would have an "uncomfortable feeling of someone watching."[21]

We may long with the poet Byron for a "society where none intrudes," but, in fact, our mutual welfare is our individual concern. How we define that welfare will continue to determine the boundaries of intimacy and intrusion in all of the areas discussed in this chapter.

Medical and Confidential

"I will respect the secrets which are confided in me." These are the words of the *Declaration of Geneva,* the international code of medical ethics adopted by the World Medical Association in 1949.[1] The principle of doctor-patient confidentiality they express is endorsed by medical associations in a majority of the world's countries, including the United States. But the practice often does not live up to the principle.

Most patients take for granted that what takes place between them and their doctors is private. In New York State the law says that "unless the patient waives the privilege, a person authorized to practice medicine, registered professional nursing, licensed practical nursing or dentistry shall not be allowed to disclose any information which he acquired in attending a patient."[2] Yet in fifteen states such information is not privileged. A physician can be forced to reveal it in court. Practitioners who refuse risk imprisonment. Nor is medical privacy completely safeguarded in all the other thirty-five states. Exceptions include compelling the doctor to describe a patient's general condition without going into specifics, allowing the physician to waive secrecy without the patient's permission, enabling relatives of the patient to force disclosure, and letting the patient provide medical details without the doctor's consent. In certain cases, although doctors' testimony cannot be compelled, their records can be subpoenaed by the court. And no federal law restricts access to medical records.

AIDS *Fuels the Debate.* The conflict between medical secrecy and the legal system has attracted particular attention recently because of the rapid spread of AIDS (acquired immunodeficiency syndrome). Since the illness first appeared in this country among gay and bisexual men and then among drug users who shared needles, AIDS has become associated in the public mind with these groups. Today, however, and in the foreseeable future, AIDS directly threatens women, heterosexual couples, and young people. The human immunodeficiency virus (HIV), which causes AIDS, is transmitted sexually, by the exchange of needles among intravenous drug users, or by the accidental introduction of AIDS-infected blood into the system either by transfusion, or through contact with open wounds.

The ways in which the condition is communicated have made it the focus of an argument concerning medical privacy in cases of rape. ''The crime of rape in the era of AIDS can carry with it a death sentence for the victim,'' according to Republican Representative Susan Molinari of Staten Island, N.Y.[3] Molinari favored federal legislation that would compel those accused of sex crimes to be tested for AIDS and would make the results of such tests known to the victim, and to the court. Since May 1991, twenty-three states have passed laws with similar provisions.

Opponents of these laws view them as "an extraordinary intrusion on the accused's right to privacy" which "clearly eliminates the presumption of innocence until an individual is proven guilty." They believe that "the mere ordering of such a test would . . . make a fair hearing difficult if not impossible."[4] And they are concerned that the victim is being misled because the results of testing the accused do not reveal if the victim has AIDS.

That's not the point, according to Representative Molinari. She worries that a victim "might not allow herself to become pregnant" because of the chance of infecting the baby, or that her relationship with her husband might suffer because of fear "that she might pass on the disease."[5] Another consideration, which Molinari doesn't mention, is that mothers with AIDS have babies with AIDS and that the prognosis for these infants is almost always poor. Knowing that the man who raped her had AIDS would allow the victim to weigh this fact in deciding for or against a first-trimester abortion.

Questions of AIDS and privacy also concern parents of school-age children. Case after case around the country has demonstrated their anxiety that the presence of a child with the AIDS virus in a classroom puts the other children at risk. However, many of the worries they express are unwarranted.

AIDS cannot be spread by spitting or using the same drinking fountains or toilets. A child doesn't catch it simply by being in the same classroom with another child who has it. On the other hand, blood from an AIDS carrier that is transmitted to an open sore can spread the virus. Parents who fear such transmission in accidents, fist fights, or simple nosebleeds are voicing a legitimate, although remote, concern.

Their concern pits the confidentiality of medical records against the need to know for reasons of public health. If the medical examination of a child entering school reveals AIDS, should the physician automatically pass along that information to school authorities? Should teachers be told so that they may take precautions to safeguard other children? Should parents be informed so they can decide if their child is at risk?

Advocates for children with AIDS claim that sharing such information causes panic among parents. They point to cases where this has driven the AIDS child from school. But there are other cases in which knowledge of the student's condition has enabled school administrators and teachers to work with the parents of other students to ease their fears and arrive at realistic safeguards for the classmates of the child with AIDS.

Some doctors are caught in the middle of this debate. Others face an even more painful moral dilemma. These are the ones who themselves have AIDS. Along with nurses, dentists, and other medical professionals similarly afflicted, they must decide whether to make their condition public and perhaps sacrifice their ability to make a living, or to keep it secret and deprive their patients of the right to make up their own minds about being treated by someone with AIDS.

These fears are mostly based on a notorious case in which a dentist kept on practicing without telling his patients he had AIDS and infected six of them with the fatal virus. This led to demands that it be made illegal for those in the medical and dental professions to withhold such information from patients. Most doctors think this is unnecessary. They point out that physicians have never been required to disclose their illnesses, although they have always been afflicted by the same maladies as the population at large. As professionals, they feel that they are qualified to take all necessary precautions to prevent the spread of AIDS if they are infected by the HIV virus.

Some AIDS organizations back up the right to privacy of doctors and other victims of the illness, but some do not. They think that alerting the public to the spread of AIDS is more important. They believe, for instance, that prominent people who contract the ailment have an obligation to make their condition public in order to help remove the stigma that the public too often attaches to AIDS. In some cases this has meant exposing a celebrity AIDS patient's gay sexual orientation as well, but the goal is to force the celebrity to lend weight to the fight against the illness.

Basketball star Magic Johnson's revelation that he had been infected with the HIV virus did indeed focus attention on the condition. Tennis champion Arthur Ashe, though, was bitter about having his medical privacy breached. In the *Washington Post* he wrote that "keeping my AIDS status private enabled me to control my life. 'Going public' with a disease such as AIDS is akin to telling the world in 1900 that you had leprosy."[6]

Four months before his death on February 6, 1993, Ashe asked this question: "To what extent is my private life not my own?"[7] Gene Policinski, sports editor of *USA TODAY*, which broke the story, answered Ashe. "When you live your life in public, you live your life in public," he pointed out. "By all the definitions of news in this country's history, what you do and what happens to you as a public figure is news."[8]

Paul Bruning of *Newsday* agreed. "Cruel as it may seem, the wishes of a stricken man cannot substitute for editorial judgment," he wrote in an article for *Maclean's* magazine. "Personal concerns are secondary to the principles of a free press."[9]

At a 1992 press conference, tennis great Arthur Ashe explained how the disclosure of his having AIDS would affect his life.

Such attitudes may explain why some doctors will not write down "AIDS" as the cause of death for celebrities on death certificates. Like some survivors of AIDS patients, they believe that the dead person's right to privacy justifies concealing, or even misrepresenting, such facts. It also saves pain for the living. Some AIDS activists deplore this on the grounds that it results in undercounting the number of AIDS cases and misinforming the public about the full extent of the threat the illness poses.

Medicine and Politics. Another area in which the public's right to know conflicts with medical privacy is politics. During the 1992 presidential campaign when then-candidate Bill Clinton lost his voice and was having obvious throat problems, leading medical journalist Dr. Lawrence K. Altman of *The New York Times* asked to interview him. Claiming his right to privacy, Clinton denied the request. *Times* columnist William Safire didn't think that was right. "The President's health," he wrote, "is the public's business." [10]

Those who agree with Safire point to the illness of President Woodrow Wilson during his last days in office, a debilitating condition that was concealed from the public while the government ran without the guidance of the elected leader. They also remind us that presidential physicians routinely lied about Franklin Roosevelt's ill health and concealed the seriousness of Eisenhower's heart condition. President Kennedy's Addison's disease, which required heavy cortisone treatment, was dismissed as a "mild adrenal deficiency." [11]

Defenders of medical confidentiality for presidents remind us that making serious medical conditions public can cause panic in the country. The news affects every area of presidential decision making. It impacts on the stock market. It paralyzes legislation. Foreign leaders respond, sometimes taking advantage of the situation. Our own foreign policy is put on hold. The effect of such news is unpredictable and perhaps dangerous.

Even if that is so, does secrecy apply to candidates as well as presidents? During the 1992 New Hampshire primary, which he won, Democratic candidate and former senator Paul Tsongas told reporters he had "fully recovered from cancer." A few months later his doctors revealed that a lymphoma had been found in his armpit in 1987. Tsongas either wouldn't, or couldn't, face how serious this was. By December 1992 he was visibly ill from cancer. In January his doctor admitted that the media should have been told about the cancerous node so that the public could have the opportunity to "come to their own conclusions." [12]

Part of the problem is the immediacy with which health bulletins are broadcast. The news often reaches the public before medical experts can analyze it. Complex diagnoses are reduced to sound bites, and these become the basis of judgment for the ordinary person. Thus privacy may not only be invaded but may also be distorted.

Some exceptions to medical privacy may be justified in the interests of an informed public. Others may be justified for other, equally compelling reasons. The problem is in knowing where to draw the line between such reasons and medical confidentiality.

Personal Records or Public Data? In 1977 the United States Supreme Court ruled on a New York State law that had set up a centralized file to record data on certain prescription drugs. These included opium, cocaine, methadone, amphetamines, and other substances for which there is an unlawful market as well as a legiti-

The 1992 presidential bid of former Massachusetts senator Paul Tsongas was plagued by concerns about his health.

mate medical use. Names and addresses of patients and doctors; frequencies of prescriptions, strengths, and dosages; and other information went into the file. The purpose was to prevent the illegal resale of drugs that had been prescribed legally.

Although many doctors and patients attacked the law as an invasion of medical privacy, the Court upheld it as "a considered attempt" to stem the flow of illegal drugs, and one that would take precautions not to violate patients' privacy interests. But the Court was careful to point out that it was not deciding "any question which might be presented by the unwarranted disclosure of accumulated private data." Writing for the majority, Justice John Paul Stevens noted "the threat to privacy implicit in the accumulation of vast amounts of personal information in computerized data banks." [13]

George Trubow, a privacy expert at the John Marshall Law School in Chicago, sees the greater threat coming from business, not government. "We've got a Constitution that limits the government," he points out. "They've got some hoops to jump through. But the private sector doesn't have any." [14]

A 1989 study by the University of Illinois confirms his apprehension. Of 275 companies selected from among the Fortune 500 corporations, 126 responded to a sixteen-page questionnaire. The 126 had a total of 3.7 million employees. As trendsetters in the world of big business, their practices in regard to medical confidentiality are representative of firms employing hundreds of millions of people.

All of the 126 companies had access to some medical information on their employees. The information came from a variety of sources, including employment applications, release forms signed by the employees authorizing doctors and hospitals to release records to the company, the results of examinations for company health plans, previous employment records, school records, and so on. The study concluded that "one-half (50%) of the companies use medical records about personnel in making employment-related decisions" while "one in five (19%) does not inform the employee of such use." [15]

Corporate executives view this as regrettable, but necessary. Their first obligation is to their stockholders. If health problems are interfering with an employee's performance, that is a valid consideration in weighing that employee's value to the company. Often, the executives point out, the company will decide that solving the problem will be better for the company than firing the employee and will provide help toward that end.

Critics say that just as often the employee with the health problem is fired, and sometimes not told why. They say that weighing performance data and health data together is neither fair nor accurate. University of Illinois professor David F. Linowes points out that "business decisions such as hiring and promotion are sometimes made on the basis of information that should never have been included in the file." He adds that "a totally unsubstantiated negative item can result in a tarnished career." [16]

Linowes's view reflects the fact that health is one of the yardsticks by which people are judged. That leaves open the big questions of just how much is entitled to be known by whom, and for what purposes? The medical professional may have to deal with these questions on a case-by-case basis, but finally it is our society as a whole that must resolve them.

Data Banks
or Dossiers?

America today is a computerized society. Government, the business community, and the average citizen all benefit from this. The storing of information in computer data banks is cheap. Data can be quickly handled and processed, saving time, labor, and money. It is no longer necessary to maintain countless file cabinets filled with records on paper. One computer chip can handle the information. Less paper is used, and so fewer trees are cut down, and this helps the environment.

But there is a danger. In his 1989 book *Private Rights, Public Wrongs: The Computer and Personal Privacy,* author Michael Rogers Rubin warned that "the various computer systems that business and government have created to keep records about people have an ever-widening reach." [1] Rubin cited a 1986 federal government report that found that these systems were "creating a *de facto* national database covering nearly all Americans." [2] This means that "bank computers can provide a personal profile of a customer's movements and activities that is more timely and detailed than one

The storage area of a computer data
company holds reel after reel of tape
containing millions of individual records.

prepared from an individual's own records" according to privacy expert David Linowes.[3]

Are personal database records eroding the privacy of citizens and their families? People who work with them say no, and cite legitimate reasons for their existence. The government, they say, has a need to gather and retain information for national security, taxation, crime prevention, redistricting, and other purposes. Government also has a stake in stimulating the economy and so shares some of this information with the business community.

Besides data provided by the government, companies themselves collect information through applications for credit, mortgages, health insurance, employment, car insurance, and the like. Forms filled out by individuals become part of their file in a data bank. The information generated is combined, updated, and shared. The file grows whenever a person contributes to an organized charity, orders from a catalog, writes to a company for information, enters a sweepstakes, answers a survey, buys a house, or even simply changes an address. (Every fourteen days the U.S. Postal Service makes available to data banks a list of people who have filled out applications to have their mail forwarded.)[4]

These data bank entries are used as the basis for "targeted marketing," the soliciting of consumers selected because the information in their files indicates probable interest in a specific product area. Businesses solicit by direct mail or telephone from lists of such potential customers, culled from the raw material of the data banks.

Computer technology makes it fast and easy to sort the names by category. When sixteen-year-old John Doe, for instance, subscribes to a skiing magazine, the information on the subscription form he filled out becomes part of his data bank file. The subscription company, which handles many magazines, rents its lists of subscribers to a list broker. The broker breaks down these lists by various categories and in turn makes them available to customers at around $75 per 1,000 names each time they use the list for a mailing.[5] Soon John Doe is receiving seasonal catalogs from sportswear companies, solicitations for vacation packages to Vermont and even Switzerland, and so forth. As a magazine subscriber, he is also repeatedly contacted by mail and telephone with offers of subscriptions to other magazines.

But how has this violated John Doe's privacy? Most marketers never see the mailing lists they use. All they are doing is trying to maximize their chance of reaching someone interested in their product. They view the activity as a service to consumers, alerting them to the availability of products in which they may have some interest. It's not illegal, and marketers see nothing unethical about it.

Knight Kiplinger, publisher of *Kiplinger's Personal Finance Magazine,* points out that "publishers exchange subscribers' names because it's the most efficient way to find new readers. And it benefits readers by holding down subscription prices."[6]

That's reasonable. Apart from a flood of junk mail and some unwanted phone calls, John Doe's privacy would not seem to be seriously damaged. However, subscribing to a magazine is only one source of the information in his data bank entry.

John Doe may have applied to a college, written away for information about acne, or joined a rifle club. In each case he will have revealed facts about himself. By the time John Doe is eighteen, his data bank entry will have been drawn from a hundred or more sources.

The danger doesn't come from any single one of these, but rather from their combined weight. An article by investigative reporter Cullen Murphy in the *Atlantic Monthly* warned that "a demographic infrastructure is being put into place in which government data, retail data, mail-order data, credit card data, banking data, medical data, and data of various other kinds are continually cross-tabulated, creating a parallel universe . . . in which our every attribute, our every wish, habit and inclination, is known and accessible."[7]

Data banks may have beneficial uses. The medical community, for instance, is able to use data banks as sources to compile and cross-index large bodies of statistical and highly technical information on a worldwide scale. Information about the spread of a disease, its causes, the conditions in which it flourishes, the success rate of various drugs used to combat it, the types of people suffering from it, and so on can be accessed, correlated, and studied in a fraction of the time possible before such data were computerized. The invasion of privacy is small when the data bank does not identify the individuals whose files have been the source of information, and it seems a small price to pay for relieving large-scale suffering.

On the other side of the question, there is the exploitation of data bank files by organizations like the Wackenhut Corporation of Florida, a security company employed by large corporations. Wackenhut, according to the *Anchorage Daily News,* was hired by the Alyeska Pipeline Service Company (which runs the Alaska pipeline and the Valdez tanker terminal) to supply information on its employees, with the goal of ferreting out company whistleblowers.[8]

Outfits like Wackenhut are known as "people hunters."[9] Corporations use them to investigate employees and competitors. Politicians use them to obtain information about opponents. Sometimes political organizations use "people hunters" to check on their own members. During the 1992 presidential campaign, some volunteers working for independent candidate Ross Perot charged that their credit had been improperly investigated by the Perot campaign. The allegation did not directly implicate Perot.[10]

New York Times columnist William Safire viewed the Perot campaign flap and other data bank incidents as examples of a major threat, which he summed up in these words: "The record of every single telephone call you make is controlled not by you, but by companies eager to cooperate with the I.R.S. Your use of credit cards offers a map to snoopers of where you go and what you spend. Your mortgage application tells marketers what you own. Your driver's license application reveals your weight to diet clubs and your cable TV contract tells the world of your interests."[11]

In Germany, the confidentiality of such information is protected by the *Datenschutz* laws. (*Datenschutz* means "data protection.") These regulations have been in force since the 1970s. They keep computer data secret. It can only be released with the subject's consent.[12]

The United States has no comparable laws. The Privacy Act, passed in 1974, was narrow in scope and only established limited procedural safeguards affecting data held by the federal government. It did give American citizens the right to see and correct government files pertaining to them. But it did not set up any mechanisms to tell people they have this right.

In 1977 the Privacy Protection Study Commission, which had been established under the Privacy Act, made numerous recommendations for legislation to the president and to Congress.[13] In 1979, President Jimmy Carter proposed a number of laws based on the commission's recommendations. As late as 1992, Congress had still failed to enact almost all of them.

Congress did pass the Computer Matching and Privacy Protection Act in 1987. Computer matching is the comparison of one data bank file against another by U.S. government agencies. "Its purpose," wrote privacy expert Jeffrey Rothfeder, "is to put the government's computers to work to rid the nation of deadbeats." In one investigation the Selective Service Administration conducted a search for eighteen-year-olds who hadn't registered for the draft by checking their files against ice cream parlor birthday lists. The 1988 act gave individuals affected by computer matching the right to contest the findings and said that information from matched files had to be independently verified. But Rothfeder concluded that "the law is just a Band-Aid" that has left victims with "a bureaucratic maze to slosh through."[14]

The courts have provided little recourse. While the Supreme Court has consistently recognized the individual's right to privacy, it has so far refused to extend that right to information about an individual once the information has been given to a third party. Following this principle, for example, the Court has ruled that when a person puts trash out for collection, it is no longer protected from unreasonable searches and seizures. In 1976 the Court ruled that information about a person's bank account was not constitutionally protected because it was held by the bank as part of the bank's business records; in 1979, it held that records of phone calls were similarly not protected.

Many privacy advocates believe the Court's reasoning was flawed in these cases. People expect such records to be private, they say, because they "reflect what we buy, where we travel, what we read, who we communicate with" and are "extensions of our selves, regardless of where they are stored."[15] Even where laws restrict access to these records, however, they are generally aimed at limiting government intrusion. Private use of the information is a separate concern.

In 1992 the House of Representatives telecommunications subcommittee wrote to various phone companies to inquire about the confidentiality of their customers' billing records. These records list the numbers of everyone the customer may have called during the billing period. One of the larger phone companies replied by citing a law that "expressly permits [us] to disclose phone records to anyone other than the government without legal process."[16] William Safire was right. Records of telephone calls are also part of the ordinary American's computer file.

One of the scariest things about such files is the possibility of error. "Computers don't make mistakes" has long been one of the boasts of the electronics industry. People, however, do. And it is people who enter the data into the files.

Data entry operators routinely record 2,000 or more transactions during the course of a working day. A typical entry may consist of a shipping number, a charge card number, a date, a merchant identification number, an inventory number identifying the purchase, and a price, as well as other information. An experienced operator can make the entry in ten to fifteen seconds.

Even the best operators, according to computer software expert Peter Brooks of Columbia University Teachers College, will make at least one error per day. Brooks adds that check mechanisms built into most systems will flag such errors and they will be corrected.

Only a very small percentage go undetected. Therefore, he estimates, the average person has only a one in one thousand chance of being the victim of such an error. This means that during a three- to six-year period, no more than one such error should find its way into someone's file. "And that error," he points out, "will as often work out to people's benefit as to their disadvantage."

Brooks concedes, however, that an input error can prove devastating. This is because when files are updated and replicated and sorted for various purposes, the error is repeated in combination with other information, resulting in a variety of interpretations of it. "The error," says Brooks, "has become that person's own personal computer virus. It can affect his or her credit rating, eligibility for health or car insurance, medical treatment, employability, etc. In that cross-indexed computer world where the file is the person, the error has become as much a part of him or her as height, weight, age, or gender." [17]

The possibility of error is one more element to add to the concerns about computer databases. Beyond the specific concerns, however, databases raise a point that each of us must decide individually: Which do we value more, progress or privacy?

The Ethics
of Drug
Testing

Do employers have the right to require employees to take urine and blood tests designed to reveal use of drugs or alcohol? Do such tests unfairly invade personal privacy? Should they be a condition of hiring or of continued employment? Where does the employee's right to privacy end and the employer's obligation to control the workplace begin? Is the business community's war against drugs really a war against privacy?

Answers to these questions must take into account an increasingly accepted interpretation of the law known as the "negligent hiring theory." [1] It says that employers are liable for crimes or mistakes made by an employee on the job if they have not adequately screened that employee for past misdeeds, mental instability, drug addiction, alcoholism, or even personality defects that might be considered dangerous. Lawrence Z. Lorber, attorney for the American Society for Personnel Administration, provides this example: "If Encyclopaedia Britannica sends a convicted rapist door-to-door the company will pay mightily in court if something goes wrong."[2]

How mightily? In a recent Maryland case the cost to a furniture-leasing company was $13 million. That's what the judge awarded the husband of a man whose wife had been murdered by an employee of the company. The firm had failed to investigate the killer before hiring him. Had they done so, they would have found that he had been convicted of armed robbery and was on parole when they gave him a job that took him into people's homes. Discussing the case, privacy expert David Linowes worries that although the business community has an obligation to see that the public "receives every reasonable and practical protection against the dishonest and criminal element in our society," the employee must be safeguarded against "abuses due to overzealousness, human error, or ignorance."[3]

The employer's legal responsibility for the employee's actions extends not only to potential customers but to other employees and to the public at large. There is also a responsibility to the company and its stockholders. The troubled employee can interfere with morale and production, cause costly accidents, affect profits. Because of such consequences, that which is personal and private is also business.

These are the circumstances behind a range of recent drug- and alcohol-abuse testing programs that many believe invade the privacy of the individual worker. The tests are used both in hiring (to screen out those with problems) and in monitoring the behavior of current employees.

Urinalysis is the most common test used. A urine sample is supplied by the subject and examined by a laboratory for evidence of drugs. Sometimes a blood test is used as a substitute, or backup. An employment

"I'm home dear . . . and you'll be pleased to know I passed the office drug test with flying colors."

NORRIS
THE VANCOUVER SUN ©

Is drug testing by employers a necessary precaution or an unwarranted intrusion? This cartoon takes the second view.

application may be rejected or a worker may be fired for refusal to take the test.

In some cases notice is given that a test will be required. In others there is no notice, on the theory that those who are habitual drug or alcohol users will then not have time to clean out their systems. Some firms' policies require that everyone in a particular work division be tested. In other companies the testing is random. And in still others workers may be selected to be tested on the basis of their productivity, behavior, dress, or lifestyle. Critics ask how fair the selection process can be when it is based on such factors. On the other hand, if everybody is tested, doesn't that constitute a wholesale intrusion in order to snare the guilty few?

While testing is usually compulsory, sometimes it is limited to the lower levels of the workforce and executives are exempt. Union leaders at General Motors have protested that such tactics are "unfairly concentrated on union members instead of management."[4] Another union issue has to do with the conditions of the test. In some companies, to be sure that the urine sample is genuine, observation of the subject producing it is required.

This may be a violation of privacy that some people simply won't allow. When her supervisor approached a California computer programmer with a glass bottle and asked her to take a urine test, the programmer refused. When she was fired the next day, she sued her employer. Her argument was that unless the company had reasonable cause to suspect her of drug use, she should not be forced to take the test. The California Superior Court disagreed. It said the employer did have the right to require the test, and the woman was not rehired.[5]

In a New York case, the State Supreme Court came to exactly the opposite conclusion. The court prohibited a local school board from testing teachers for drug use on the grounds that "an invasive bodily search may be constitutionally made only when based upon supportable objective facts."[6] The federal courts also seem to be leaning toward considering forced drug testing "an invasive bodily search.''[7] And in 1992, the Third Circuit Court of Pennsylvania ruled that a "fired employee can sue over drug testing.''[8]

The American Civil Liberties Union, which supported that decision, has called for new and stronger laws to protect the privacy of American workers both on and off the job.[9] Nor are they alone in being concerned about the increased use of drug testing by employers. The *National Law Journal* warned as far back as 1986 of "massive drug screening . . . by about one-quarter of the leading industrial companies" of "nearly five million persons" over a twelve-month period.[10]

In the University of Illinois study cited in chapter 5, 58 percent of the 126 Fortune 500 companies who responded had substance-abuse testing programs. Nine out of ten used drug testing to screen potential employees. Testing was compulsory. The average number of tests conducted by each company over a twelve-month period was 772.[11] A 1988 survey of more than a thousand companies by the American Management Association reported that two thirds of manufacturing companies and 38 percent of service firms tested their employees.[12] Neither proponents nor opponents of testing argue with the fact that drug testing by employers has increased since then.

In recent years, a series of tragic accidents would seem to justify the increase. There were 5 deaths and 171 injuries in the August 1991 wreck of a subway train at the Union Square Station in New York City. The motorman who drove the train was later convicted of manslaughter and received a five- to fifteen-year jail sentence. He had admitted to drinking heavily before driving the train that fatal night and to falling asleep at the controls.

More than a year earlier, in March 1990, three peo-

Twisted wreckage of a New York City subway car shows the force of the 1991 derailment that killed five people.

ple died and many more were injured in a subway crash in Philadelphia. The motorman driving that train had used cocaine. And in January 1991, there was evidence of drug use by an engineer involved in a train crash in Corona, California.

Drugs have taken their toll in other areas as well. A study by the National Transportation and Safety Board released in 1990 concluded that drugs, including alcohol, were involved in a third of fatal truck accidents in the United States.[13] Later that year *The New York Times* reported that a survey of job screening results linked drugs with workplace accidents as well as with absenteeism.[14]

As the evidence has piled up, there has been pressure for still more testing. In August 1991, spurred on by the tragedies in New York and Philadelphia, there were congressional demands for increased and tougher drug and alcohol testing in mass-transit systems, which until then had been exempt from conducting routine tests. The president of the Transit Workers Union of America dropped his opposition to drug testing. In December 1992, the U.S. Transportation Department proposed that transportation workers routinely be given breath tests for alcohol.

Motormen, engineers, airline pilots, truckers— these are people who perform jobs where lives are at stake. Arguably, they have an obligation to be drug-free and sober. And arguably, their employers have a duty to make sure that they live up to that obligation. The same could be said of manufacturing jobs where the safety of many employees may hinge on one worker's drug-and-alcohol-free performance. Does logic demand the same for all jobs where productivity and profitability require teamwork, and where an addiction-weakened link might undermine a company to the point of failure and thereby cost co-workers their livelihood? To some people, these considerations justify the invasion of privacy by drug and alcohol testing.

Not everybody thinks so. Some experts believe that the invasion of privacy is particularly unjustified because drug testing, in their opinion, doesn't really work. They cite studies that found a high rate of false results. Tests could not tell the difference "between the morphine injected by an addict and the morphine absorbed from poppy seed rolls" or came up with the same positive rating for "someone who had just snorted cocaine and for someone who recently drank an unlabeled over-the-counter herbal tea containing fragments of coca leaf." [15] These experts note that prescription drugs, over-the-counter drugs, and some food components can cause a person's urine to test positive for illegal drugs. Even inhaling substances from the atmosphere may cause a test to be positive. This creates the "potential for thousands of [innocent] people testing positive from urine tests." [16]

That is what happened to twenty-four police recruits in Washington, D.C. They were part of a group of thirty-nine suspended when tests indicated they had used drugs. All thirty-nine names were identified in the media as marijuana users. But the test was faulty, and twenty-four recruits were reinstated. [17] Those against testing point out that not only was the privacy of the innocent recruits invaded, but as a result of that invasion, false information about them was made public. In a similar case in 1990, the New York City Transit Authority paid out $5.6 million to 1,800 employees who had been the victims of faulty drug tests. [18]

A small percentage of faulty tests, however, may be offset by a hidden advantage. Company executives see testing "as a good deterrent to drug use." Drug and alcohol abuse costs American business over $175 billion a year in absenteeism, lost productivity, and accidents. If the effect of testing, regardless of accuracy, is to reduce that figure, then the testing programs are worthwhile.[19]

This viewpoint has generated "a $300 million-a-year industry for businesses producing urinalysis kits and operating diagnostic labs."[20] Privacy advocates see a danger in this industry exaggerating the drug and alcohol threat to produce still more business. They point out that under our system of law, each person is presumed innocent until proven guilty. Drug and alcohol testing turns that around, assuming that those tested are guilty until proven innocent. They say the tests go far beyond the workplace to expose private leisure-time activity. Employers, they protest, are equating poor job performance with substance abuse although there is no hard evidence to show that people who drink or use drugs after hours are less productive than those who abstain.

There is support for this position. In a dispute involving the Greyhound Bus Lines and its drivers, the arbitrator ruled that Greyhound could not require drivers to stop using marijuana in their leisure time. "Workers in society," the arbitrator proclaimed, "are free men and women, with the fundamental right to live their lives as they choose."[21]

It is a decision that alarms test proponents. They point out that if a bus driver who is trusted by passengers with their lives cannot be tested to make sure that he or she is drug-free, then the public has no protection at all. There must be safeguards for people—for passengers, customers, other workers, the company and its stockholders, and the public at large. The right to privacy must not be held higher than the right of all of us to be safe from the effects of drugs taken by others.

Professor Linowes is among those who believe that viewpoint "is wrong morally." He has written that those who espouse it are "ignorant of the consequences of personal-privacy abuses, including their own."[22] He speaks for many privacy advocates who see testing for substance abuse as eroding a fundamental right of United States citizens.

There is no dignity for the individual without privacy, says one side, and drug and alcohol testing threatens that privacy. There is no peace for society without security, says the other, and drugs threaten that security. Somewhere between those two views lies the compromise necessary to preserve both security and privacy.

Youth and
Privacy

"Adults have always tried to regulate teenagers' private lives," points out author Janet Bode, who has met with thousands of high school students in the course of writing books dealing with many of their most sensitive problems. "The limits may vary from one generation to the next, but the issue of privacy is always there. Some teenagers agree to the rules. For those who don't, the battle is on. Testing limits is part of *becoming* an adult. Part of *being* an adult is guiding and protecting the young. To do that, adults infringe on teenagers' privacy to some extent. That's the nature of being human."[1]

For young people, the issue of privacy begins at home. Parent-child relationships involve both love and power. Love means concern with the welfare of the child; power is the expression of that love by physically safeguarding the child. The baby's hand is pulled back from the flame, the toddler is restrained crossing the street, the six-year-old is kept from gorging on candy, the ten-year-old is not allowed to ride a bicycle in heavy traffic. And the fourteen-year-old is forbidden to drink liquor, smoke pot, or be promiscuous.

How far should restraints go? Recently a Miami plastic surgeon invented a homing device to track children. It would be implanted behind the child's ear and emit a signal monitored by a cellular telephone.[2] Some view the invention as a good way to keep tabs on children. Others see it as a direct threat to their privacy.

The Teen Years. By the teen years, the limits of privacy have been regularly extended. Parental intrusion eases off as minors take more and more responsibility for themselves. However, the teen years bring new and different pitfalls. Many parents feel the same duty to protect their offspring from these dangers as from earlier ones. Others simply cannot break the habit of exercising power over their children.

Do parents have the right to invade their minor children's privacy for the children's own good? If they do, just how far should that right extend? How far does it extend legally?

The answer varies from state to state, and sometimes from case to case. Courts tend to grant parents wide latitude to intrude in their children's lives, except where parental authority is exercised with violence. The laws do not specifically protect the privacy of children from encroachment by their parents.

In any case, the legal issue is not what is addressed in most families. Perhaps the most common issue from a teenage perspective is deciding when parental concern is genuine, and when the parent is just locked into a power trip. This question is at the core of the teen-parent struggle over privacy. Some of the elements of the struggle are serious and some are trivial. But the emotions aroused on both sides are often deeply felt.

Drug use among young people has made the privacy issue more difficult for them and for their parents. In 1990 the introduction of a spray kit called DrugAlert focused debate over the issue. DrugAlert consisted of three aerosol sprays that turned color when they came into contact with surfaces touched by drugs. The idea was for parents to spray the desks, books, or personal possessions of teenagers to determine if they were using controlled substances.[3]

DrugAlert raised hard questions for those concerned with privacy as a civil liberties issue. There was no legal barrier to it because it was designed for parental use, rather than for use by a law enforcement agency or some other outside authority. But privacy advocates, including Loren Siegel of the American Civil Liberties Union, deplored its use because it preyed on parental fears rather than addressing real problems of drug use by minors. The American Broadcasting Company refused to run an ad for DrugAlert; director of programming Art Moore said, "Basically we felt it was an invasion of privacy."[4]

Privacy is a high priority for teens. Psychologists agree that with puberty comes a need for more space and more privacy. Teenagers need an area of their own, a space on which others can't trespass. They need privacy in which to grow up. But that isn't always possible. Many teens have to share space with siblings, parents, or other family members. Situations vary, but often teens have to carve out areas of privacy for themselves and fight fiercely to maintain them.

Lisa, who is grown now, remembers her need for privacy as a teenager. "I kept a diary," she recalls, "and put the most personal things in it. Not just events in my life, but fantasies, too. It was pretty steamy stuff, I guess, and I lived in fear that my mother would dig it out from where I hid it and read it. So I wrote things on the beginning pages about how much I hated my mother and how nosy she was and what an awful person she was. I guess I figured that would shock her so she wouldn't read any further. Actually, I loved her and she didn't intrude on my privacy as much as a lot of my friends' mothers intruded on theirs. Once, after I was grown up and out of the house, I asked her if she had ever read my diary. She just smiled."[5]

Parents aren't the only, or even the most frequent, intruders into a teenager's privacy. Often siblings are. Younger children who may want nothing more than to emulate a brother or sister may invade privacy in a quest for information that will help them do that. Older siblings may act out of genuine concern, or may simply be on their own power trip.

The difference is that parents can exercise authority. Parents may invade their children's privacy in an effort to prevent unwise behavior or establish limits that teens may not establish for themselves.

Such efforts extend into other areas affecting privacy. Parents may restrict reading materials and movies because they glamorize smoking, drinking, taking drugs, violence, or sex. They may forbid music with lyrics that are offensive, suggestive, or disrespectful of others. They object to companions they perceive as bad influences, or to anything they feel violates the values they have worked hard to instill in their children. Parents may intrude on what would otherwise be private decisions in these areas because they feel that the teenager isn't ready to make these decisions, and that for his or her own good control must be exercised.

It is not always even-handed. Author Janet Bode points out that "despite any recent gains in equality between the sexes, teen females still have less privacy than males.''[6] In her book *New Kids on the Block: Oral Histories of Immigrant Teens,* Bode quotes a sixteen-year-old who summed up the 1990s limits parents lay down for females with these words: "Be careful when you go out. Open your eyes and close your legs. Study hard to get good grades. Have a career.''[7]

Teens often greet such parental advice with skepticism. It seems out of touch with real life. And in fact, the advice does not seem to be very effective—at least not where sex is concerned. United States teenagers have one of the highest pregnancy rates in the Western world—double that of England, France, and Canada. Some 50 percent of unmarried females between the ages of fifteen and nineteen have had sex. The figure goes up to 60 percent for males in the same age group.[8]

It may be that the legal system will adjust to this before parents themselves do. In July 1992, Florida Judge Jerry Lockett ruled that the statutory rape law forbidding sex between minors under age fifteen and adults over age eighteen violated the privacy rights of the minors.[9] His decision, however, has no effect on other states and may not survive review by a higher court. If it should prevail, it will surely increase the pressure on some concerned parents to monitor their children.

In chapter 4 we discussed the question of parental notification before a minor is permitted to have an abortion. One argument against it is the fear that the teenage female has of punishment by a parent who has forbidden her to have sex in the first place. The parent has foreseen consequences that the teenager has chosen to ignore. But does the teenager have the right to make that choice?

Desire may be a private feeling more powerful than morality, but should it be more powerful than safety? With teenagers at risk from AIDS and other sexually transmitted diseases, don't caring parents have a duty beyond morality to try to keep them from the dangers of having sex? Isn't that more important than their children's privacy?

Privacy in School. Regardless of the answers, parental intrusions on teen privacy lead inevitably to other invasions. These are justified by a legal doctrine known as *in loco parentis,* meaning "in the place of a parent," which refers to "a person acting temporarily with parental authority." It applies to all teachers and supervisory personnel responsible for students while they are in school.

Originally, *in loco parentis* meant that students had no privacy rights recognized by school authorities or by the courts. That interpretation was redefined by the U.S. Supreme Court on February 24, 1969. The case was *Tinker* v. *Des Moines Independent Community School District.*

Tinker was not specifically about privacy. However, the wording that decided it established a principle followed in many subsequent cases where privacy was the issue between students and school authorities. The facts in *Tinker* were as follows:

On December 16, 1965, Mary Beth Tinker, a Quaker student in Des Moines, Iowa, was suspended along with two fellow students for wearing black armbands to school. The armbands were meant to show support for a suggestion by Senator Robert Kennedy that there be a Christmas truce in the Vietnam War. Because feelings about the war ran high, school authorities felt that the armbands might be disruptive.

But there had been no disruption, only the fear that there might be. The Supreme Court decided in favor of the students. They pointed out that they had not "shed

*Mary Beth Tinker, with her mother
and younger brother Paul.*

their constitutional rights to freedom of speech or expression at the schoolhouse gate.'' They added that ''in our system state-operated schools may not be enclaves of totalitarianism. School officials do not possess absolute authority over their students.'' [10]

That last sentence quoted was what pushed open the door for students to challenge the right of school officials to infringe on their privacy. But it did not mean that they had no authority, only that the authority was not absolute. In fact, teachers and school administrators do have considerable leeway legally to interfere with students' privacy. As Professor Thomas I. Emerson of Yale Law School has noted, "the fortunes of students who seek to vindicate their rights through the judicial system have varied." He adds that "at the lower level of the educational structure the rights accorded students tend to diminish."[11]

There is obvious justification for a kindergarten student not having the same rights to privacy as a high school sophomore. But just as in the home, the privacy rights are extended as the student progresses through the grades. Usually the question that comes up with students in their teens is just how far.

The answer varies from school to school and from courtroom to courtroom. There is no single legal precedent, for instance, that spells out how far teachers can go in interfering with the private right of students to choose what they wear and how they groom themselves. The courts have not really clarified the issue since 1971, when the American Civil Liberties Union defended a female high school student who had been suspended for not wearing a brassiere under her clothing.[12]

Regulating females' personal clothing choices was common even at the college level as late as 1964, when women at New York City's Queens College (including graduate students in their late twenties and early thirties) were subject to rules forbidding the wearing of slacks, pants, or jeans even in the coldest weather. At the high school level the 1960s brought a spate of dress codes in reaction to student activism. Hair length was a particular target.

In 1966, in Dallas, Texas, three male teens were forbidden to enroll in a local high school because they wore their hair long. They were members of a rock 'n' roll group, and style was important to their image. The ACLU sued the school board on their behalf, claiming that "forcing students to conform to a particular hair style violated the right of privacy that is implied in the Bill of Rights." The case went as far as the United States Court of Appeals for the Fifth Circuit, which ruled against the three students on the grounds that freedom to choose one's own hair style was not as important as "maintaining an effective and efficient school system."[13] In other words, long hair was a distraction to other students and interfered with the learning process. The court suggested that the boys cut their hair and wear wigs when they performed.

Two years later an opposite decision was reached by the United States Court of Appeals for the First Circuit in the case of a Marlboro, Massachusetts, male student suspended for refusing to cut his shoulder-length hair. The "concept of liberty," the court affirmed, includes "the right to wear one's hair as he wishes."[14] And in an Oregon case involving an honor student suspended for growing a mustache in his senior year, Judge Robert C. Belloni commented that he couldn't "conceive of any disciplinary problems or disruption . . . because a boy wears a mustache." And he added this statement: "In fact it seems to me that unreasonable and arbitrary rules imposed by those in authority are themselves the causes of disciplinary problems."[15]

There are educators who view such statements as naive, or insulting, or both. In their view, some styles of grooming and dress are disruptive and should be banned. They see it as a matter of the right of the majority of students to be educated without distraction. In one school where gold chains (many of them imitation) were a status symbol among male students, a principal banned them on the grounds that more attention was being paid to them than to lessons. In another case, male students were forbidden to wear single earrings because they provoked catcalls. High-style sneakers, designer jeans, and decals have been forbidden, skirt-lengths mandated, and makeup restricted in other schools.

Dress codes are sometimes instituted to prevent violence. If male members of two rival gangs wear shirts emblazoned with their gangs' symbols to class, it creates an atmosphere of apprehension regardless of whether or not actual fighting breaks out. Other students cannot be expected to function well in such an atmosphere, according to some school administrators.

When New Jersey principal Joe Clark drew up a high school suspension policy, it included a five-day suspension for wearing hats in school. One of his teachers questioned the wisdom of such punishment for what seemed to him a minor infraction. Principal Clark answered him with these words: "Ghetto youths have been murdered because of the hats they were wearing. Murdered because someone else desired the tall, silly leather thing or the big colorful woven thing. And murdered because the hat identified the youth as a member of a particular gang."[16]

Teen gangs do complicate the problems of drugs, alcohol, weapons, and vandalism in the schools. Increasingly strict measures are being employed to deal with them. These include both wholesale and selective searches of students' lockers, briefcases, pockets, and purses; body searches; hidden cameras; and urine tests. Many of the protections adults have against such invasions of privacy are not available to minors. They were taken away by a 1985 Supreme Court decision that reestablished much of the power of *in loco parentis* diluted by the Tinker case.

In the 1985 case, a female student was caught smoking in a New Jersey high school bathroom. She was brought to the office of an assistant principal who took her purse, opened it, and searched it. He found drug paraphernalia and a small amount of marijuana. Taken to the police station, she confessed that she had been selling drugs at school. When she went to trial, her attorney claimed that the search of her purse had been an illegal violation of her privacy rights.[17]

In deciding the case, the Supreme Court commented on the growing drug use and violence in schools. They said that while completely arbitrary searches were not allowed, school authorities were not subject to the same restrictions limiting searches as police were. For instance, the Court said, a teacher or principal did not have to obtain a warrant before searching a student's property, or the student, because that would hinder "disciplinary procedures needed in the schools." All that was required was that such searches be "reasonably related" to the original reason for them.[18] In effect, this established an exception to the Fourth Amendment prohibition against unreasonable searches and seizures. The Jersey student lost her appeal, and the decision greatly narrowed the privacy rights of all students.

In its wake, body searches for weapons have become daily occurrences in many inner-city high schools. So have locker searches and probes for drugs. However, while urine testing has been used to detect drug and alcohol use in many schools, at least one state, New Jersey, has affirmed the rights of students not to submit to them.

A Rutherford, New Jersey, school added a urine test for drugs to the yearly physical examination required of all students. The school board said there would be no civil or criminal charges against any student who tested positive. They said the program was fair because nobody was singled out. Every student's

Locker searches—for guns, drugs, or other banned substances—have become routine in some schools.

urine was tested. New Jersey Superior Court Judge Peter Ciolino decided the policy was unconstitutional because it invaded the students' privacy. He accused the school of attempting "to control student discipline under the guise of a medical procedure" that "violated reasonable privacy expectations of school children."[19]

The decision leaves some educators caught between a rock and a hard place. One aspect of *in loco parentis* is that it makes school districts and schools liable if a pupil is injured. If a student on drugs becomes violent and hurts another student, the injured one's parents can sue the school and the individual principal or teacher for not having taken reasonable precautions to safeguard their child. For school personnel, discipline, not privacy, is the more pressing problem. With much of the public agreeing, strong measures have been implemented around the country.

In August 1990, in Tazewell County, Illinois, a drug raid on all of the county's high schools resulted in all of the students being held in custody while the privacy of many was violated by searches.[20] And in March 1992, in the town of New Ipswich, New Hampshire, the Mascenic Regional High School installed videotaping cameras in students' bathrooms as a means of dealing with vandalism and graffiti.[21]

Such anti-privacy measures are extreme. Less so, but also of concern, are frequent breaches of confidentiality of school records. Included in these records are academic ratings, psychological evaluations and test scores, health information, comments by teachers and counselors, family background data, and descriptions of behavior patterns. The Buckley Amendment to the federal Elementary and Secondary School Act of 1974 gave parents the right to view and challenge these records and in some cases have them corrected. Students do not have that right in many states unless they are over eighteen years old.[22]

The privacy of records varies widely from state to state. While California allows parents to see all their children's records, Connecticut holds back material related to counseling sessions. Texas will release records to educational personnel and spouses of students. Colorado opens the files to employers and police. In Tennessee the data may be made available to researchers. In Oklahoma, a teacher who intentionally discloses school records to anyone but a parent may be guilty of a misdemeanor, while New Jersey has few limitations on such disclosures. Nebraska separates academic records from disciplinary records, which are destroyed after graduation if a student requests such action.[23]

Nebraska's policy points up the need for confidentiality. Without it, a teenage indiscretion can follow a person from job to job over a period of years. Thus the privacy right denied to minors can affect their entire life. A student's "permanent record" can be very permanent indeed.

These varying policies show that for teens, privacy is a juggling act, with minors having to balance their rights against the responsibilities of those who have authority over them. All-out rebellion against teachers or parents is counter-productive. Their power can only be challenged successfully on the basis of reason and ethics. However, that does not mean it should never be challenged. As Iowa State Senator Richard Varn, principal sponsor of a bill affirming rights for Iowa students, has pointed out, "Students can't learn about fundamental rights and freedoms unless they are allowed to use those rights."[24]

Many teens believe that the right to privacy is the most precious right of all.

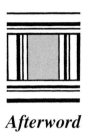

Afterword

As we have seen, the right to privacy is not absolute, but relative. It must be treasured, carefully safeguarded, but sometimes it must be redefined, sometimes compromised. The future will present privacy dilemmas we can only dimly perceive in the present. Progress is not just a matter of technology, but of philosophy and ethics as well. What will your values be in the many areas that impinge on privacy, and how will you apply them?

You will be most severely tested by intimate issues. With the number of adults revealing that they were abused as children continuing to grow, privacy in the home will be a major battleground. The question of notification of parents of minors seeking abortions will not go away. Neither, given the growing popularity of X-rated videos, will privacy clashes involving censorship and pornography. Privacy issues concerning sexual orientation will spill over from the military into other areas, and the ethics of ''outing'' will continue to be disputed.

Medical privacy will be a persistent problem. To-morrow's doctors, dentists, and nurses will be faced with increasingly more complex issues of confidentiality. They will have to decide between the privacy rights of the individual patient and the need to compile data useful in fighting disease. If a cure for AIDS is not found, they will be in the middle of the battle between the privacy rights of patients and the rights of others to information they believe necessary to protect themselves or their children. They will be part of the debate over the public's right to know the medical condition of political candidates and incumbents. They will have to decide how much information to release about a polyp or a cancer, or whether to make available the particulars of a presidential heart attack or stroke.

Such issues will involve the media as well as the medical establishment, and they will concern all future citizens. Communications theorist Marshall McLuhan stated that "the medium is the message." His point was that the news on television is not only being reported, it is being shaped by the technology relaying it and by the format in which it is presented. It may seem obvious to say that a crime story on a printed page is different from a crime story on a TV screen, but the implications of that difference—and of the impact on the privacy of the people in the story—will be a major future concern.

Already, true crime TV mini-dramas re-enacted by actors for the entertainment of prime-time audiences are overwhelming the privacy of victims, survivors, and perpetrators. Once they have become news, the law does not safeguard people. Will the future change that? Will limitations be imposed?

Will an informed public continue to be more important than the individual's privacy if the news media develop new mechanisms to be more intrusive than ever before? Will executions be covered live on the late-night news? Will rape victims be identified as a matter of course?

There are no signs that violence will decrease over the coming years. Public insistence that crime be controlled will grow along with it. That will surely have an impact on privacy. The next generation will have to decide whether or not to support demands that emerging technologies—video telephones, more and more easily accessed data banks, automatic-tracking zoom-lens camcorders, electronic signaling devices, laser telephone taps and bugs—conform to law enforcement needs. Laws will have to be re-examined with an eye toward accommodating new crime-fighting inventions. Tomorrow's courts will have to decide between the exclusionary rule and the threat of "good faith" exceptions eroding privacy safeguards. Hard questions will have to be answered regarding the privacy of crime victims, the rights of defendants, and the requirements of prosecutors.

With negligence suits becoming more and more of a business expense, and the reasons for them increasingly traced to drugs and alcohol, the pressure for mandatory drug testing is sure to mount over the next decade. With testing also becoming more common in schools, such questions as pre-notification versus surprise tests, wholesale testing of employees versus random testing, or testing based on behavior, dress, and lifestyle will have to be considered.

Restrictions on access to computer databases will be considered. Legislation may be needed to control the limitless spread of personal information. Licensing and supervision of list brokers will be deliberated. It may be necessary to define information by category and to place some of the categories beyond the reach of those who break down lists in order to target markets. Decisions will be made on limiting the intrusiveness of telephone and direct-mail solicitations. Future legislators will scrutinize the activities of "people hunters" to determine what privacy controls are needed. The sharing of information by government with the business community may have to be curtailed. Germany's *Datenschutz* laws may be adapted to conditions in America. Telephone records must be safeguarded and a mechanism devised so that computer errors can be corrected and replication prevented.

These are difficult problems. Some of them have been faced by the present generation. Some have been avoided. None, however, have been resolved. Now is not too early to start thinking about how to resolve them.

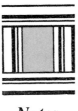

Notes

Chapter 1

1. Paul Bender, "Privacy," in *Our Endangered Rights: The ACLU Report on Civil Liberties Today,* ed. Norman Dorsen (New York: Pantheon Books, 1984), p. 238 (quoted from *Olmstead* v. *United States, 1928).*
2. David F. Linowes, *Privacy in America* (Urbana and Chicago: University of Illinois Press, 1989), p. 1.

Chapter 2

1. Author's interview with Howard Rushmore, 1959.
2. *New York Newsday,* January 8, 1993.
3. "Total Exposure: Privacy and the Press," NBC telecast, October 8, 1992.
4. CBS newscast, May 1992.
5. *New York Newsday,* September 19, 1992.
6. Paul Bender, "Privacy," in *Our Endangered Rights: The ACLU Report on Civil Liberties Today,* ed. Norman Dorsen (New York: Pantheon Books, 1984), p. 241.
7. *Time, Inc.* v. *Hill* (1967).
8. Norm Goldstein, ed. *Associated Press Stylebook and Libel Manual* (New York: Associated Press, 1992), p. 292.

9. Gay Talese, *The Kingdom and the Power* (New York: World Publishing, 1969), p. 373.
10. "Total Exposure."
11. "Total Exposure."
12. "Total Exposure."
13. "Total Exposure."
14. Elder Witt, ed. *The Supreme Court and Individual Rights* (Washington, DC: Congressional Quarterly, Inc., 1980), p. 65 (quoted from *Wolston v. Reader's Digest Association, Inc.,* 1979).

Chapter 3

1. Witt, p. 169 (quoted from *Wolf* v. *Colorado,* 1949).
2. Stanley N. Katz, "An Historical Perspective on Crises in Civil Liberties," in *Our Endangered Rights: The ACLU Report on Civil Liberties Today,* ed. Norman Dorsen (New York: Pantheon Books, 1984), p. 320.
3. David Rudovsky, "Criminal Justice: The Accused," in Dorsen, p. 209.
4. *New York Newsday,* September 12, 1992.
5. *The New York Times,* September 18, 1992.
6. Jerry Berman and Janlori Goldman, *A Federal Right of Information Privacy* (Washington, DC: The Benton Foundation, 1989), p. 5 (quoted from *Katz* v. *United States,* 1967).
7. Witt, p. 182.
8. *The New York Times,* January 15, 1993.
9. *The New York Times,* January 15, 1993.
10. *Wall Street Journal,* November 12, 1990; and *The New York Times,* January 10, 1993.
11. *Wall Street Journal,* November 12, 1990.
12. *Wall Street Journal,* November 12, 1990.
13. *Wall Street Journal,* November 12, 1990.
14. *Wall Street Journal,* November 12, 1990.
15. Warren Freedman, *The Right of Privacy in the Computer Age* (Westport, CT: Quorum Books, 1987), p. 122 (quoting *The Universal Declaration of the Rights of Man,* UN Doc. A/180).

Chapter 4

1. Eve Cary, *Woman & the Law* (Skokie, IL: National Textbook Company, 1981), pp. 184–187 (quoting from *Roe* v. *Wade*, 1973).
2. Cary, pp. 189–190 (quoting from *Planned Parenthood of Central Missouri* v. *Danforth*, 1976).
3. *The New York Times*, January 22, 1993.
4. Cary, pp. 189–190.
5. *The New York Times*, January 22, 1993 (citing *H. L.* v. *Matheson*, 1981).
6. Ibid (citing *Hodgson* v. *Minnesota*, 1990, and *Ohio* v. *Akron Center for Reproductive Health*, 1990).
7. *The New York Times*, January 22, 1993.
8. *The New York Times*, January 22, 1993 (quoting from *City of Akron* v. *Akron Center for Reproductive Health*, 1983).
9. *The New York Times*, January 22, 1993 (quoting from *Thornburgh* v. *American College of Obstetricians and Gynecologists*, 1986).
10. Paul Bender, "Privacy," in *Our Endangered Rights: The ACLU Report on Civil Liberties Today*, ed. Norman Dorsen (New York: Pantheon Books, 1984), p. 253.
11. Bender.
12. Bender.
13. Bender (quoting from *Griswold* v. *Connecticut*, 1965).
14. Elder Witt, ed., *The Supreme Court and Individual Rights* (Washington, DC: Congressional Quarterly, Inc., 1980), p. 274 (quoting from *Griswold* v. *Connecticut*, 1965).
15. Wendy Kaminer, *A Fearful Freedom: Women's Flight from Equality* (New York: Addison-Wesley Publishing Co., 1990), pp. 178–179.
16. *Los Angeles Times*, April 4, 1992.
17. Kaminer.
18. Edward De Grazia, *Girls Lean Back Everywhere: The Law of Obscenity and the Assault on Genius* (New York: Random House, 1992), p. 537.
19. De Grazia, p. 537.
20. *The New York Times*, January 27, 1993.
21. *The New York Times*, January 27, 1993.

Chapter 5

1. *Encyclopaedia Britannica,* 1970, vol. 15.
2. Warren Freedman, *The Right of Privacy in the Computer Age* (Westport, CT: Quorum Books, 1987), p. 57 (quoting *New York State Civil Practice and Law Rules,* Section 4504).
3. Susan Molinari, "Victims First," *New York Newsday,* January 6, 1993.
4. H. Alexander Robinson, "Justice Last," *New York Newsday,* January 6, 1993.
5. Molinari.
6. Fred Bruning, "How a Private Citizen Lost His Privacy Rights," *Maclean's,* May 4, 1992, p. 13.
7. "Total Exposure: Privacy and the Press," NBC telecast, October 8, 1992.
8. "Total Exposure."
9. Bruning, p. 13.
10. William Safire, "Clearing Clinton's Throat," *The New York Times,* January 14, 1993.
11. Safire.
12. *The New York Times,* January 17, 1993.
13. Paul Bender, "Privacy," in *Our Endangered Rights: The ACLU Report on Civil Liberties Today,* ed. Norman Dorsen (New York: Pantheon Books, 1984), p. 248 (quoting from *Whalen* v. *Roe,* 1977).
14. Wayne Biddle, "They've Got Your Number," *The Nation,* October 26, 1992, p. 470.
15. David F. Linowes, *Privacy in America* (Urbana and Chicago: University of Illinois Press, 1989), p. 40.
16. Linowes, p. 61.

Chapter 6

1. Michael Rogers Rubin, *Private Rights, Public Wrongs: The Computer and Personal Privacy* (Norwood, NJ:, Ablex Publishing Corp., 1988), pp. 73–74.
2. Rubin, p. 68.
3. David F. Linowes, *Privacy in America* (Urbana and Chicago: University of Illinois Press, 1989), p. 110.

4. Kristin Davis, "How They Got Your Name," *Kiplinger's Personal Finance Magazine*, April 1992, p. 46.
5. Davis, p. 44.
6. Davis, p. 44.
7. Cullen Murphy, "Force of Numbers," *The Atlantic*, July 1992, p. 20.
8. Wayne Biddle, "They've Got Your Number," *The Nation*, October 26, 1992, p. 468.
9. Biddle.
10. *The New York Times*, January 3, 1993, and January 4, 1993.
11. William Safire, "Peeping Tom Lives," *The New York Times*, January 4, 1993.
12. Biddle, p. 467.
13. Rubin, pp. 87–88.
14. Jeffrey Rothfeder, *Privacy for Sale* (New York: Simon & Schuster, 1992), pp. 140–146.
15. Jerry Berman and Janlori Goldman, *A Federal Right of Information Privacy* (Washington, DC: The Benton Foundation, 1989), p. 7.
16. Biddle, p. 467.
17. Author's interview with Peter Brooks, January 30, 1993.

Chapter 7

1. Jeffrey Rothfeder, *Privacy for Sale* (New York: Simon & Schuster, 1992), p. 171.
2. Rothfeder.
3. David F. Linowes, *Privacy in America* (Urbana and Chicago: University of Illinois Press, 1989), pp. 160–161.
4. Linowes, p. 15.
5. Warren Freedman, *The Right of Privacy in the Computer Age* (Westport, CT: Quorum Books, 1987), p. 64.
6. Freedman.
7. Freedman.
8. *The National Law Journal*, June 1, 1992.
9. *Christian Science Monitor*, December 28, 1990.
10. Freedman, p. 64.
11. Linowes, pp. 40 and 52.
12. *Personnel* magazine, May 1989, p. 39.

13. Washington *Post,* February 6, 1990, and *Los Angeles Times,* February 6, 1990.
14. *The New York Times,* November 29, 1990.
15. Ronald K. Siegel, *Intoxication* (New York: E. P. Dutton, 1989), p. 291.
16. Linowes, p. 36.
17. Linowes, p. 36.
18. *Village Voice,* February 2, 1993.
19. Siegel, p. 292.
20. Linowes, p. 14.
21. Linowes, p. 37.
22. Linowes, p. 16.

Chapter 8

1. Author's interview with Janet Bode, January 1993.
2. David F. Linowes, *Privacy in America* (Urbana and Chicago: University of Illinois Press, 1989), p. 21.
3. *The New York Times,* September 13, 1990.
4. *The New York Times,* September 13, 1990.
5. Author's interview with Lisa K., January 1993.
6. Author's interview with Janet Bode, January 1993.
7. Janet Bode, *New Kids on the Block: Oral Histories of Immigrant Teens* (New York: Franklin Watts, 1989), p. 97.
8. Statics on teenage sexuality and pregnancy rates compiled by the Alan Guttmacher Institute from sources including the Centers for Disease Control and Prevention, the Center for Population Options, the National Center for Health Statistics, and the National Academy of Sciences.
9. *The New York Times,* July 25, 1992.
10. Barbara Habenstreit, *Eternal Vigilance: The American Civil Liberties Union in Action* (New York: Julian Messner, 1971), p. 139.
11. Thomas I. Emerson, "Academic Freedom," in *Our Endangered Right: The ACLU Report on Civil Liberties Today,* ed. Norman Dorsen (New York: Pantheon Books, 1984), p. 188.
12. Habenstreit, p. 23.
13. Habenstreit, pp. 140–141.

14. Habenstreit, pp. 140–141.
15. Habenstreit, pp. 142–143.
16. Joe Clark and Joe Picard, *Laying Down the Law* (Washington, DC: Regnery Gateway, 1989), pp. 42–43.
17. John Sexton and Nat Brandt, *How Free Are We?* (New York: M. Evans, 1986), pp. 250–251.
18. Sexton and Picard.
19. Warren Freedman, *The Right of Privacy in the Computer Age* (Westport, CT: Quorum Books, 1987), pp. 82 and 106.
20. Nat Hentoff, Washington *Post,* August 18, 1990.
21. *The New York Times,* March 25, 1992.
22. Freedman, p. 15.
23. Freedman, p. 106.
24. Nat Hentoff, *Free Speech for Me—But Not for Thee* (New York: HarperCollins, 1992), p. 360.

Major Court Decisions

(Cases heard by United States Supreme Court, except as noted.)

1914   *Weeks* v. *United States* spells out the exclusionary rule, an important privacy safeguard.

1928   *Olmstead* v. *United States.* Supreme Court Justice Louis Brandeis's dissent defines privacy as "the right to be let alone." This definition strongly influenced subsequent Court decisions.

1958   *NAACP* v. *Alabama* finds a basis for the right to privacy in the First Amendment.

1965   *Griswold* v. *Connecticut* establishes the privacy of the marriage relationship, rendering many laws that attempted to regulate it invalid.

1967   *Katz* v. *United States* extends Fourth Amendment protection to persons, not just places, in finding warrantless wiretapping to be unconstitutional.

1968   *Ferrell* v. *Dallas Independent School District* (United States Court of Appeals for the Fifth Circuit) says male high school students have no privacy right to refuse to cut their hair if the school administration requires it to maintain discipline.

1969   *Tinker* v. *Des Moines Independent Community School District* extends constitutional rights to high school students.

Stanley v. *Georgia* confirms right to read or watch obscene material in the privacy of one's own home.

1970   *Richards* v. *Thurston* (United States Court of Appeals for the First Circuit) extends the right of privacy to a male student's right to wear his hair as long as he pleases.

1973   *Roe* v. *Wade* recognizes a right of personal privacy encompassing a woman's decision to terminate her pregnancy.

1976   *United States* v. *Miller* holds that people do not have constitutionally protected privacy rights to personal records held by a bank.

Planned Parenthood of Central Missouri v. *Danforth* confirms a woman's right to have an abortion without her husband's consent and, in the case of a minor, without parental permission.

1977   *Whalen* v. *Roe* upholds a state's right to maintain a central file on patients' prescriptions as a weapon in the war against illegal drugs.

1979   *Bellotti* v. *Baird* weakens *Danforth* and gives parents a qualified veto over a minor's decision to have an abortion.

1981   *H. L.* v. *Matheson* further weakens *Danforth*, giving states authority to require that doctors inform a minor's parents before performing an abortion.

1985   *Odenheim* v. *Carlstadt-East Rutherford Regional School District* (Superior Court of New Jersey) decides that forcing high school students to undergo urine tests for drugs is unconstitutional because it violates their privacy.

New Jersey v. *T. L. O.* gives school authorities the right to search students' property and persons without a warrant if they have a reasonable suspicion the search will yield illegal drugs or weapons.

1986   *Patchogue-Medford Congress of Teachers* v. *Board of Education* (New York Supreme Court) prohibits state agencies from drug testing personnel.

Bowers v. *Hardwick* says homosexuals can be prosecuted for performing certain acts committed in the privacy of their bedrooms.

Thornburgh v. *American College of Obstetricians and Gynecologists* strikes down the Pennsylvania Abortion Control Act of 1982 requiring that a woman seeking to terminate a pregnancy must first be given information phrased to discourage abortions.

1990   *Hodgson* v. *Minnesota* and *Ohio* v. *Akron Center for Reproductive Health* give a state the right to compel a pregnant teenager to notify one parent of her intention to obtain an abortion as long as there is an alternate provision allowing her to get permission from a judge.

Osborne v. *Ohio* excludes child pornography from the right to read or view obscene material in the privacy of one's own home.

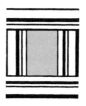

For Further Information

Recommended Reading

Dorsen, Norman, ed. *Our Endangered Rights: The ACLU Report on Civil Liberties Today.* New York: Pantheon Books, 1984.

Faux, Marian. *Roe v. Wade: The Untold Story of the Landmark Supreme Court Decision That Made Abortion Legal.* New York: Macmillan Publishing Company, 1988.

Freedman, Warren. *The Right of Privacy in the Computer Age.* Westport, CT: Quorum Books, 1987.

Glasser, Ira. *Visions of Liberty: The Bill of Rights for All Americans.* New York: Little, Brown and Company, 1991.

Gross, Beatrice, and Ronald Gross. *The Children's Rights Movement: Overcoming the Oppression of Young People.* Garden City, NY: Anchor Press/Doubleday, 1977.

Linowes, David F. *Privacy in America: Is Your Private Life in the Public Eye?* Urbana and Chicago: University of Illinois Press, 1989.

Rothfeder, Jeffrey. *Privacy for Sale: How Computerization Has Made Everyone's Private Life an Open Secret.* New York: Simon & Schuster, 1992.

Siegel, Ronald K. *Intoxication: Life in Pursuit of Artificial Paradise*. New York: E. P. Dutton, 1989.

Organizations to Contact

ABA Center on Children and the Law, 1800 M Street NW, Washington, DC 20036

Alcoholics Anonymous General Service Board, 468 Park Avenue South, New York, NY 10016

American Society of Criminology, 1314 Kinnear Road, Suite 212, Columbus, OH 43212

American Civil Liberties Union, 132 West 43 Street, New York, NY 10036

American Medical Association, 515 North State Street, Chicago, IL 60610

Center for Constitutional Rights, 666 Broadway, New York, NY 10012

Center for Media in the Public Interest, 455 West 56 Street, New York, NY 10019

Children's Defense Fund, 111 Broadway, New York, NY 10006

Citizens for Media Responsibility Without Law, P.O. Box 2085, Rancho Cordova, CA 95741

The Alan Guttmacher Institute, 111 Fifth Avenue, New York, NY 10003

National AIDS Clearinghouse, P.O. Box 6003, Rockville, MD 20849

Private Citizen, Inc., P.O. Box 233, Naperville, IL 60566

Society of Medical Jurisprudence, P.O. Box 1304, New York, NY 10008

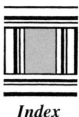

Index

Page numbers in *italics* refer to illustrations.

DATE DUE

HIGHSMITH   # 45102